The Apple Tree

Lynette Sofras

Published by Inspired Romance Novels
ISBN-13: 978-0615639727 ISBN-10: 0615639720
First Edition, 2012
Published in the United States of America
Contact info: contact@inspiredromancenovels.com
http://www.inspiredromancenovels.com

CHAPTER ONE

"Julie? Little Juliet Somerville! I don't believe it. Can it really be you?"

Julie had been busy dodging the lunchtime crowds but halted at the hearty exclamation and firm hand grasping her elbow. The force of this wheeled her bodily towards the voice. Impatient pedestrians, forced to stop in their tracks before sidestepping the pair, clucked their disapproval. She turned to her assailant, blinking as recognition dawned.

"Robert! What a lovely surprise!"

Robert returned her smile and Julie scanned his face, searching for the inevitable changes etched by the passage of time.

"What a blast from the past, as they say." He tilted his head to one side. "How many years has it been?"

She laughed. "I don't know. Five or six, I suppose. It's so nice to see you, Robert. How are you?"

"Five or six? Closer to eight I should say. We must celebrate...you're not too busy, I hope?"

"Not at all. Just idling. I'd like that."

He took her arm in a brotherly fashion and led her towards the nearby Crown Inn. "Now let me think," he began after procuring drinks and settling himself beside her on the claret-colored banquette, new to the Crown since Julie's last visit. "The last time I saw you would be when you went up to university. I haven't seen Lizzie in almost as long, although I hear she's doing okay for herself."

"Yes," Julie conceded, although he was wrong about the date. They'd met again the following year, at her father's funeral, but perhaps Robert's memory was being tactfully selective. "Liz has just been appointed as consultant at the hospital. Father would have been extremely proud of her."

"Yes, of course. And of you too no doubt—where are you working now?"

"I'm not at the moment. I suppose I'm what actors fondly call 'resting'. But never mind that...tell me about yourself," she urged, eager to change the subject.

"Me? I'm doing very well, thanks. I have my own garden center now, down on Longshore Road, and the business is doing pretty well." Robert would have been unable to conceal the note of pride from his voice even if he'd tried. "We're doing more and more landscape gardening these days—I've got six full time staff and several part-timers. You must come and see the place, now that you're home."

"Of *course* I will," she assured him. "And are you married?"

He paused, replacing his drink on the table and eyeing it for a brief moment before replying. "I was, yes. I married Linda Henderson—I don't think you knew her. But she died." He uttered this last statement with the brutal simplicity of someone who still found the subject acutely painful.

"Oh how awful! I'm so sorry. Can you...I mean, would you rather not...?"

"I don't mind talking about it. It was quite a while back, you know—over four years now. A traffic accident...she was killed instantly...and she was...we were..." He gave a little cough to clear the thickness in his throat and took a small sip of his beer. "She was pregnant at the time, so we lost the baby, too."

Julie gasped and stared at him.

"It was bad at first, of course. We'd only been married eighteen months. I suppose I fell apart a bit, but time and good friends have helped. And the work, of course. I couldn't have managed without that."

"Poor Robert." She'd known him for as long as she could remember. They had been neighbors and he and her older sister, Liz, were school friends. He always seemed to be present, somewhere in the backdrop of her childhood memories, always smiling, always cheerful. Good old Robert. Imagining him 'falling apart', in pain and suffering while she got on with her own life somewhere else in the world, was difficult. No stranger to the anguish of death, she might have done something useful for once in her little life if she'd known. A tear formed in the corner of her eye and spilled onto her cheek, but whether this was for Robert or herself, she made no attempt to analyze.

Robert, whose remaining speech had gone unheard by Julie, evidently saw the tear and jumped rapidly to his own conclusions.

"Don't cry, little Julie. As I said, I've made peace with it now. I'm over it. Scout's honor!" And like a good scout, he drew a clean white handkerchief from his pocket and dabbed at the tear, before handing the square of cloth to Julie. She looked at it and then at him.

He was so transparent. Her tears probably touched his simple vanity. Robert had always believed her to be too soft and vulnerable for the tough world of medicine and had told her as much years ago. He'd also said it saddened him to see her succumbing to the wishes of her father and sister. Of course, she'd been young and naive enough to believe that just wanting something sufficiently was enough to guarantee success and set the whole world to rights.

"Come on, now, this is supposed to be a celebration. Tell me about your life. Has some lucky, handsome doctor snapped you up, yet?"

Julie dabbed at her face with the soft handkerchief. What percentage of men still carried handkerchiefs? Was it the last sign of a true gentleman or merely an indication that Robert was never destined to make the transition into the twenty-first century? She grimaced inwardly at her frivolous thoughts and shook her head, so Robert might be forgiven for reading this gesture as a response in the negative to his question.

"Of course not...too busy forging a name for yourself in medical history, just like Lizzie, eh?" he said.

Julie smiled. How typical of him to assume she should follow in her sister's successful footsteps. Elizabeth had never professed any interest in marriage, being, in a sense, married to her busy career. But Julie was in no mood to discuss the complexities of her failed marriage and aborted career and accepted his easy dismissal of the subject gratefully and without contradiction.

This was a behavioral trait of Julie's that was in danger of becoming a habit. It mimicked an early form of denial, this taking refuge behind the mistaken assumptions of others rather than setting things to right by exposing the truth. Psychologists or behaviorists might label it a weakness. Julie preferred to view it as the easiest way out of a tricky confrontation. But she felt a nagging guilt nevertheless. Characteristic or weakness, she had to acknowledge that old friends always deserved the truth.

"I really am very sorry about your wife. I wish I'd known. But then, Liz never tells me anything. She's so cut off from the world by her work and research, and now this new clinic—she might as well be on another planet!"

"That's understandable. Liz is a very selfless woman, she always was."

Robert was understanding to a degree that he actually sounded pompous. His curious choice of adjective bemused her. Selfless? What did that mean? The opposite of selfish? Hardly, not Liz! Yet it was a curiously apt word to describe her older sister who, at thirty-five and a strikingly attractive woman, had probably never paused longer than three seconds in front of a mirror to look at herself. Julie always thought that if anyone asked Elizabeth to describe herself physically, she would probably not even know the color of her own eyes intimately. She was far too preoccupied with her career to gaze at her own reflection. She was the Mother

4

Theresa of medicine—cardiology, to be more precise. Mother Elizabeth...Saint Elizabeth...

"So you must come to dinner and meet her," Robert implored, gazing earnestly into Julie's face as she returned to the present with a guilty jolt. So engrossed in her musings about her sister, she'd caught nothing but the tail-end of his speech.

"Yes of course." She agreed then worried about her eagerness. "I mean thanks! I should like that very much."

"Excellent. I know you and Sonya will like each other. Shall we say Thursday, then? About eight?"

"Yes, that's fine." Who might Sonya be and what else had Robert said? She could hardly ask him to repeat himself.

"You're staying with Liz, I presume? Are you home for good? You've barely told me anything about yourself," he reproached, perhaps just a little sheepishly, in the way that people who monopolized conversations often did.

"I have no definite plans at the moment. Yes, I'm at home with Liz for now. I've been living and working in London, but I spent the last year in Saudi Arabia."

"Saudi? Good grief!" He raised his eyebrows in surprise. "Working?"

"Well, yes...but I was pretty miserable there. I'm just relieved to be home again," she added quickly, hoping that he wouldn't pursue the subject further.

He didn't and they conversed on subjects of a far more general nature for a further ten or fifteen minutes until the throaty hum of his cell phone, vibrating in one of his pockets, reminded him of his afternoon meeting and they took their leave of each other.

"Until Thursday, then." He handed her a small business card. "Addresses, phone numbers, everything you need is on here. Unless you find time to call in at the nursery before then."

"Oh, I certainly intend to do that," she assured him, before their final parting. And she meant it.

On the sidewalk outside the Crown Inn, Julie watched Robert's departing back until the purposeful lunchtime crowds swallowed him up. In her current state of lonely wretchedness, she felt his departure acutely. He represented an umbilical link with the 'triple s' of her childhood— safety, security and simplicity. He was a link with her mother and the uncomplicated bliss of childhood...with ponies and poetry and fun and flowers. And on top of those treasures, he had absolutely no connection with the more recent past and the confined, suffocating world of medicine that had dominated her life for almost a decade.

After her brief bout of self-indulgent wallowing, Julie continued on her own purposeless way, treading time, trying to get a step ahead of the decisions that were threatening to engulf her yet again.

Conversation with Elizabeth on anything other than medicine had always been a trial. Cardiology was her pet subject and with the clinical aspects of the heart, she was in her element, but the emotional vagaries of that organ were beyond her understanding. Liz had always taken an interest in Julie's career, ensuring that she should not deviate from the central road of medicine onto the rockier path of surgery.

When Julie met and soon afterwards married Simon Gardiner, during her final year of medical school, Liz worried he might lure Julie into the surgical network. But if Simon had tried, he would have failed spectacularly. Without his tireless help during her six months of surgery, she would certainly have failed to complete her pre-registration year altogether. So fundamentally convinced was she that she had chosen the wrong profession, she would have abandoned her career then and there. Since taking a break from both career and husband, those feelings returned more forcefully than ever.

Liz reproached Simon in his absence for his benightedness in marrying Julie too soon and in taking her off to Saudi Arabia so early in her medical career. Liz had never seen eye-to-eye with Simon, doubting his motives and resenting his intrusion from the outset. After all, she was in a far better position to help her sister in her career than some surgeon from the south of England.

"At least your year in Saudi Arabia must have allowed you plenty of time to study for the exam," Liz observed. She was referring to the all-important Membership examination for the Royal College of Physicians.

Julie steeled herself to reply. "Actually, Liz, I don't think I shall bother with it."

"Not *bother*? What on earth do you mean?"

"I'm thinking of throwing it in."

"Throwing *what* in?" Liz demanded, as if they no longer shared the same language.

Julie sighed. "Medicine, Liz. The more I think about it, the more I feel I've made a terrible mistake. I just don't want to be a doctor."

"Nonsense! You *are* a doctor. Unless you mean that you're back on that silly flirtation with surgery? He's not persuaded you to take up surgery, I hope?"

Julie shook her head. This friendly rivalry between physicians and surgeons and their comical name-calling had always amused her, though she had never taken sides in the opposing factions. To her mind, they all worked equally for the common good and neither specialty was superior. "No, of course not. I mean altogether. Give up medicine completely. I don't want to be a doctor, Liz!"

Possibly for the first time in her life, Julie's sister had no reply. She stared, as if seeing Julie for the first time. As though she might be some alien being. Blinking, she recovered herself enough to articulate her thoughts. "You must be insane! Very well...so your marriage fails...these things happen...but, Julie, for goodness sake..."

"Perhaps we could discuss it another time?" Julie said to avoid, yet again, the detour down the path of failed marriages.

"Nonsense. We must discuss it here and now. What would my poor father say?"

"He was *my* father too." Julie knew that must sound sulky and childish. "And I think if he were alive now, I'd be able to make him understand." There has to be someone, somewhere who can understand that I just want *out*, she thought wretchedly.

"Understand? But he's not here to understand anything, which is why we have a duty to respect his wishes. How could you consider abandoning medicine when that was his dearest wish for you?"

"Was it?" Julie's voice broke. "Are you quite sure it was *his* wish, Liz? Only sometimes, I wonder why any father would want to put his daughter through such torment. Yes, you heard. I hate medicine. I always have. I hate dealing with human misery, with sickness, pain and fear. And I know I'll *never* be a good doctor."

Liz surveyed her sister at length before replying. "Look, Julie, I do believe this business with Simon has upset you far more than you led me to understand. You're right—we should postpone this discussion for a week or two. You'll feel differently after you've had a good rest."

Several weeks passed quietly for Julie, as Liz made no attempt to resume the discussion. New text books appeared on her desk at regular intervals, which she idly perused but her mind absorbed little information. Julie felt woolly-headed and detached from the world of medicine now that it was no longer part of her daily routine. However, it surrounded her and engulfed her. She admitted, though only to herself, that before ever she could put it behind her, she must first confront it.

Eventually Liz brought up the subject again. "I presume you have entered for the May exam...I'll quiz you tonight, if you like?"

Julie had *not* entered her name for the May examination, nor did she feel equal to a night of 'quizzing' from her sister. "Liz, I'm sorry! I haven't been studying. I just can't manage to organize my thoughts properly at the moment. But I promise I'll enter for the November exam. And I'll study." Even as she said the words, she regretted them. She had merely said what she knew Liz wanted to hear, to buy a little peace for herself for just a few extra weeks.

Mollified, Liz smiled. "Of course you can do it if you put your mind to it. Now I think we ought to start thinking about a job for you. Dr Richardson's rotation is coming up shortly. Of course he'd prefer someone with at least a passing interesting in endocrinology, but I think I might manage to..."

"No job! Please! I don't want to work just yet. Don't worry about me. Just leave me alone and I'll sort things out for myself. I don't want to be organized any more. Let me do things my own way."

But left to her own devices, she failed to sort out anything. She managed to devote an hour or two of each day to studying but was in a constant state of agitation — a fever to be out of the house, driving or rambling through the countryside on long solitary treks or wandering the town gazing absently into shop windows. It was on one of these excursions that she'd encountered Robert Ashley.

The Thursday of her dinner engagement with Robert and the mysterious Sonya found Julie driving along Longshore Road.

R Ashley
Nursery & Landscape Gardening
Marquee Hire and Container Planting

The sign in buttercup-yellow letters on a green background caught Julie's attention and she pressed on her brake and swung between the tall gates into the broad, semicircular drive which afforded ample space for cars. At the center of the arc squatted a wide, low, glass-fronted building with an abundance of greenery in the windows. To the right of this was a low, rambling building, boasting on a blue and white sign 'Inside-Outside Marquees' with a second door displaying the word 'Cornucopia' in multi-colored letters. To the left of the main building was a newer construction, smaller still and in the final stages of completion, but this had no sign to explain its function. A vast array of terracotta in all shapes and sizes lined the driveway, glowing warmly in the pale sunlight and lending a faintly continental feel to the place. Fronting the smaller building, a motley assortment of statues, ponds, trellises, fountains and a huge quantity of garden ornaments continued for some distance behind it.

As Julie drew closer to the main building, gazebos, pagodas and other such incongruous dwellings appeared in the vast stretches of land to the rear. She peered through the jungle of greenery in the central building but could detect no sign of life. Entering the cool and dim interior, she allowed her eyes to adjust slowly in the bosky gloom.

A man emerged from an open doorway, wiping his hands on a square of cloth. Dressed in denim, his jeans tightly fitting, shirt open at the neck and with rolled up sleeves, all very workmanlike, he surveyed her, tilting his head slightly to one side. He was perfect. In spite of her natural reserve, she stared at him openly, unable to draw her eyes away from the sight in case it faded back into greenish ether. His eyes, keen and clear, met and returned her gaze coolly. And still her eyes refused to drag themselves away.

"Can I help you?" he asked at last, a flicker of a smile playing about his lips.

It was then Julie remembered to close her mouth and start breathing again. She gave herself a mental shake, a kind of pulling herself together exercise, and a strange, though not at all unpleasant tingle rippled across her skin. The exercise worked. She even managed a fairly normal-feeling smile. "I was looking for Robert. Robert Ashley. Could you tell me where I might find him?"

A frown creased his forehead and she resisted the urge to reach out and gently smooth it away, restoring the face to its former perfection. "He's not here, I'm afraid. He's over at Nettlesby this afternoon. Have you tried his mobile? We don't normally open on Thursdays," he explained.

It was Julie's turn to frown. She felt in her pocket and drew out Robert's information-packed card, scrutinizing it closely. There it was, in small print *Early closing: Thursday*. She tapped her fingertips against her forehead. "How stupid of me. I'm sorry."

"It's not a problem. But as I'm here, maybe I can help?"

Julie shook her head. "Oh no. But thank you. Robert suggested I might call in when I was passing and have a look around. I should have checked his card. Silly of me. I'll come back another day."

His attractive face broke into a smile and Julie couldn't help smiling too. It was involuntary, like the thrill she had felt as a child when the Christmas lights were switched on for the first time. His smile was every bit as delightful as those twinkling, colored lights to a child's eyes. "Well, as *I'm* here, why not let *me* show you around?"

And of course she protested and a polite verbal fencing match began, each objection swiftly and skillfully parried until she gave in with gratitude and good grace and allowed herself to be conducted through cavernous greenhouses and long rows of hothouses sheltering exotic architectural plants, through shrubberies, orchards and tiny model gardens, while her good-looking guide answered her questions and drew her attention to anything worthy of more than a passing glance, like the external root system of some exotic palm.

His exquisite hands mesmerized her as he pointed things out. She had always thought Simon had attractive hands—typical surgeon's hands, she used to call them— but she loved the way the gardener lovingly caressed the plants with his long, sensuous fingers as he spoke. She felt a tiny tingle of pleasure and half-expected to see golden fingerprints or new life blossom wherever he touched. 'Green fingered' didn't nearly do justice as a description.

"You seem to get great satisfaction from all this," she remarked as they made their way back to the main building via 'Cornucopia' which turned out to be an area devoted to hanging baskets and decorative container planting.

"Yes I do. I find it very therapeutic working with plants. I only wish I could spend more time here."

"Oh? Then you don't work here full-time?" She'd already determined from his mannerisms and speech that he was unlike any gardener she had ever come across. He must be one of those part-timers Robert mentioned. She wondered what else he did. He was too old to be a student, surely?

He laughed at her question. "Oh no. I wish I did. I'm just a casual helper."

A casual helper, working the half-holiday for a little extra overtime perhaps? He might lose even this tenuous position if Robert returned and found him wasting time with her instead of working. She wanted to help and a thought struck her suddenly. "My sister's always complaining about the state of our garden. I wonder if you could use some extra work—in your free time?"

He frowned, looking more baffled than annoyed. "Gardening?" He sounded hesitant.

"Or landscaping" she added quickly. "I mean whatever you think necessary. I'm sure there's a huge scope for improvement. We have someone come in a couple of times a month but it's all he can do just to keep it tidy. And you could fit in the hours to suit yourself so that you don't lose time here." The words tumbled out and she realized she must sound far too eager. She was throwing herself at him in the most blatant and uncharacteristic way. *Damn, it Julie, get a grip!*

His frown was replaced by a smile of such evident amusement that it threatened to turn to laughter. "Well, I'm not sure that I could take on such a big job personally, but I'd be happy to take a look and offer suggestions. A low-maintenance garden." He considered it for a moment. "That could be good practice for me."

Not take it on personally? But it was a gift! What did he *do* when he wasn't working for Robert? "Oh yes, and then you could give us your quote." How lame, but she wanted to make it clear she meant paid work, not a favor. He probably thought she was too pushy. Her cheeks burned at what must seem like her eagerness to provide him with work. "Not, of course, that I can foresee any problems in that respect." *Oh help. Dig, dig, dig. What is this hole I'm digging for myself?* She drew one of Elizabeth's cards from her purse and handed it to him.

"'Dr Elizabeth Somerville'," he read aloud.

"That's my sister," she explained. "I'm Juliet, though everyone calls me Julie."

His smile broadened. "And I'm Nicholas...Masserman." He offered her one of his exquisite hands to shake. She took it, savoring the thrill of touching those beautiful, long, sensitive fingers with her own. Perhaps he was a writer or an artist who merely tended gardens for pleasure or to supplement his income? She still held his hand and he gazed at it with that same quizzical amusement that threatened to erupt into laughter. She released it quickly.

"Would Saturday afternoon suit you, Miss Somerville?"

"What?"

"To look over the garden?"

"Oh yes, of course! That would be perfect. And it's Julie, remember?" He placed the card in the back pocket of his jeans and she felt a twinge of guilt at her deliberate deception. Perhaps she should have said Julie Gardiner, not Somerville—Dr Somerville, maybe, but Mrs Gardiner, in the eyes of the law. She had removed her wedding ring many weeks ago.

Like many married professionals, she'd retained her maiden name after marrying Simon. As they both worked in the same hospital, it avoided confusion. But that was in the medical world. To tradesmen, she was Mrs Gardiner.

"Julie," he repeated, as if trying it out for size. "And would you like to leave a message for Bob? I'll be seeing him around six."

"Oh no. I'll be seeing him tonight myself. I'm invited to dinner to meet his, um..." She faltered at the realization that she had forgotten the name of Robert's mysterious friend.

"Sonya," he volunteered.

"Oh yes, of course. Sonya. Maybe I should take some flowers." She glanced around at the cut flowers crammed into so many pots and vases.

"For Bob or Sonya?" His voice sounded teasing, amused.

She looked back, unsure how to reply. Was Sonya her hostess or not?

"I really shouldn't bother," he assured her. "She always has a house full."

Julie frowned. That suggested that Sonya lived with Robert, but if she didn't, then bringing flowers might seem a bit presumptuous on her part. As well as stupid! The man owned the nursery—why would she bring flowers from *his* business to his house? And why hadn't she listened properly to Robert the other day?

"Perhaps flowers aren't the right thing...a bit...inappropriate?" she murmured unhappily.

"Not *inappropriate*," he corrected, "just unnecessary. And as I'm staying at Bob's house myself, I'll be seeing you again tonight as well."

"You are?" She blinked, unable to think of any suitable reply because of the multitude of feelings rampaging her senses. Things were certainly looking up, but she felt suddenly exhausted, as if she was taking part in a play for which she'd received the wrong script. She turned towards the display of house plants. Good breeding has well-established roots. She ought to buy *something*. Randomly she selected an interesting-looking indoor palm.

"My sister adores these," she lied, doubting Elizabeth had any affection at all for house plants. He took the plant from her and proceeded, unskillfully, to wrap paper around its terracotta pot. "How long have you been lodging with Robert?

He wrestled, all fingers and thumbs, with the sticky-tape dispenser. "A few years. Since Linda died. I trust you know about that?"

"Yes, he told me." She handed him a twenty-pound note. Did she dare tell him to keep the change? No, better not. He might be offended. He had to turn a key and tap a code into the cash register, evidently getting it wrong, as the machine beeped in complaint and stubbornly refused to open. Julie had to look away to hide her amusement. She remembered Robert's words about time and good friends helping him over his bereavement and felt irrationally pleased to think that this Nicholas with the sensitive hands was one of those 'good friends'.

"Thank you again for the tour," she said.

He reached around her to open the door for her just as her hand touched the handle. For the briefest moment his hand covered hers and he smiled at her. He insisted on carrying the plant to the car and she unlocked the back door.

"My pleasure." He wedged the palm on the floor at the rear and tested it to ensure it was secure. "I look forward to seeing you again later."

She smiled and nodded, thinking, and *that*, I can assure you, is *entirely* mutual.

Leaving the garden center, she continued along Longshore Road for a mile or so before turning right towards the town center, stopping to buy chocolates and wine for the evening. She hoped that Sonya would not also have a house full of chocolates or be one of those permanent dieters. And then, on a sudden impulse, Julie stepped inside an elegant and very expensive-looking dress shop.

CHAPTER TWO

Sonya was a tall and rather formidable-looking woman of indeterminate age, though Julie guessed her to be about thirty. An untameable mass of brown curls teased a face too asymmetrical to be described as beautiful, but still appealing because of her large eyes, softened by kindness and her ever-smiling mouth.

Her rather strident voice was a bit disturbing and she seemed unusually enthusiastic about meeting her guest and striking up a friendship with her.

"I've heard so much about you and your family, so it's nice to finally meet someone who knew my Robert as a child. Was he an obnoxious brat?" Sonya actually winked at Julie, startling her.

"Not at all." Julie fought to overcome her natural reserve. "He was one of the best."

"Told you!" Robert linked arms with the pair of them and led them towards two voluptuous blue sofas flanked by matching armchairs. "My past is an open book, but of course she doesn't believe that and will try to wheedle all sorts of new information out of you if you're not careful." He was grinning like a ventriloquist's dummy.

"Well I doubt I know any of his secrets." After all, why should I? Julie thought. "I was too much in awe of him as a child." She smiled but Sonya's easy familiarity somehow put her at a disadvantage.

In contrast to Julie's shyness and slightness of stature, Sonya appeared Junoesque, but despite her loud voice and welcoming nature, there was a self-assuredness and inner calm about her which Julie found appealing. Sonya appeared to be a perfect match for Robert. How did she compare with the dead Linda though?

Nicholas had been right about plants being superfluous. One of the walls appeared to be comprised entirely of foliage. Julie also heard the rhythmic trickle and splash of water on shingle emanating from the wall. There must be some sort of indoor fountain among the greenery.

Introductions made, Julie relaxed, more at ease with the unaffected couple before Nicholas made his appearance. Dressed all in black, he looked even more stunning than earlier. The thoughts and feelings that coursed through her body shocked Julie, never having experienced such a thrill of sexual attraction to anyone before. *This is pure animal lust—the same kind Lady Chatterley felt for her gardener!* That thought made her shriek inwardly. *Interior hysteria!*

"Ah yes," Sonya cooed. "We hear you've already met our Nicko."

Nicholas extended his hand to her for the second time that day. She noticed his well-manicured and scrubbed nails. Definitely an artist's hands, she thought.

"Yes, Mr Masserman very kindly showed me around the garden center this afternoon..." She stopped suddenly, fearing she may have said the wrong thing and jeopardized his job. Nicholas only smiled.

"It's Nicholas," he corrected. "Nick, if you prefer."

But not *Nicko*, thank goodness.

He helped himself to a drink before gracefully folding his lean frame into a rather low armchair placed at an angle to her chair. Robert began to fire questions about his garden center and whether

Nicholas had omitted anything from his tour. She was able to reassure him unequivocally on both scores and Robert appeared satisfied at last while Nicholas laughed at the compliment.

"And I hear you're a doctor like your sister and father. Genius must run in your family." Sonya once again took the lead. Nicholas raised his eyebrows—it was his turn to be impressed—as Sonya continued. "What an exciting life you must lead."

"Far from it, I assure you," Julie said with a self-deprecating laugh that bore no trace of humor.

"And I don't believe you. I mean, you've just returned from Saudi Arabia. How can that compare with our humdrum little lives?" Sonya persisted.

A sinking sensation dragged at her insides. She didn't want to think about the past year, in fact, it was the last subject she wanted to discuss with anyone right now. From whichever angle she viewed it, it reminded her of her failure.

Saudi had been Simon's idea. With his own future success guaranteed, a break in Saudi suited him and Julie had viewed it as an escape route and jumped at the move. Too quickly. She believed it would be a place with space to breathe, to recoup, to discover herself and re-evaluate her future. But it had been nothing like that. As much as Simon enjoyed his life there, she hated it. Yet another mistake.

She shifted her unhappy gaze to her hands, which still held her glass of vodka and tonic. A cube of ice cracked and splintered into smaller lumps, which proceeded to chase each other around the glass. How odd. It wasn't until the liquid sloshed that she realized her hand shook. With surprisingly good timing, Nicholas pulled a small drinks table between their seats and set his own glass down, as if to demonstrate how it should be done. At the same time, he politely asked which part of Saudi, as if it was of no real consequence.

She looked straight into his eyes. "It was near Riyadh, and to tell the truth, I was pretty unhappy there. I'm very glad to be back in England."

"Sonya comes from Australia, originally," he said in reply before Sonya could speak again. "And like all Aussies who travel, she's done the seven continents and seen all the wonders of the modern world." His accent became more mock-antipodean with every word. Sonya was the first to convulse. "But you ask her and she'll tell you what she's always telling us. There's nowhere like dear old England anywhere else in the world, possums." This last was uttered in a perfect Dame Edna mimic and somehow, in the general merriment that followed, the subject of Saudi Arabia was sidelined and forgotten.

From that time on, it was an evening of almost undiluted hilarity and enjoyment. Julie finally stopped resisting the magnetic pull of Nicholas's proximity when she realized with thrilling clarity at some point in the evening that the attraction was almost certainly mutual. Every time she moved her head, they made eye contact and with each fresh little smile they exchanged, another layer of resistance peeled away.

But the conversation over dinner left her feeling uncomfortable and guilty, threatening to spoil her pleasant evening. The topic was marriage—Sonya and Bob's wedding in the autumn. And as sometimes happens, given the idiosyncrasies of human nature, the subject of marriage pretty soon turned to its opposite state—divorce, which drew from Nicholas such a powerful polemic as to render Julie breathless with surprise. Not so, Sonya, who was evidently familiar with Nicholas's views on divorce.

"We all know your views on *that* subject, Nicko," she said amid peals of laughter and then turned to Julie and said in an exaggerated stage whisper, "For such an enlightened, twenty-first century bloke, he's more old-fashioned than my *grandfather!*" Then addressing the table in general, "But you need have no fears on my account, Nicko. When Roberto takes me for his wife, he'll be stuck with me for the rest of his life."

Julie looked down at her plate, experiencing a sudden stab of irrational dislike for Sonya. How could the woman be so *gauche*? And where did this irritating, seemingly-affectionate, pseudo-Italian habit of rounding off everyone's name with an "o" fit in to things? Before the evening was out, she might have to respond to the name *Julio!* And why was Sonya so self-deprecating, as if she could barely believe her luck in finding a man to marry her? But as these thoughts coursed through her brain, Julie felt ashamed. The reason for her irritation stemmed from her own feelings and a vague, uneasy sensation of guilt.

She looked up and caught Nicholas's eye, not too difficult to do by this stage! "As one in three marriages end in divorce, statistically that means if we all get married, then one of us around this table will end up divorced."

"Not if you marry Nicky," Sonya pointed out with a whoop of delight that almost crucified Julie with embarrassment. Robert and Sonya had to support each other through their mirth. When she was able to raise her eyes again, Julie saw Nicholas trying to hide his own amusement as he watched her struggle to justify her views. *Dig, dig, dig. Will I ever get out of this hole?*

"You seem to have very strong views on divorce," she accused.

"I certainly do. The rising divorce statistics you referred to reflect all that's bad about our disposable society, in my opinion. It's the root of all the social and economic problems of our day..." A mock groan from Sonya interrupted his words.

"Not the rubber gloves brigade," she teased.

"And the lowering of standards caused by cheap fashions which allow people to slip in and out of marriage like disposable knickers," Robert put in.

Shocked and mystified by the banter, Julie looked on silently. Nicholas sat back watching the little charade unfold as though he had heard it all before.

"People shouldn't be allowed just to slip in and out of marriage," Sonya said.

"As they do a set of clothes," added Robert.

"Like rubber gloves."

"Or disposable knickers."

"Such people ought never to be allowed to marry in the first place," they chorused in unison.

Nicholas clapped, halting the performance. To Julie's relief, he did not appear annoyed by this friendly mockery of his beliefs. If someone had attacked Simon's views in such a way...here the speculation broke off, for she was unable to imagine how Simon might have responded. She turned to Nicholas. "Surely you allow for human error? Sometimes people simply make mistakes."

Nicholas shook his head. "One should never make mistakes 'simply'. But most people are too shallow and impatient to give sufficient consideration to the real meaning of the marriage contract and as soon as they encounter difficulties, off they run to consult their solicitors. Which accounts for the appalling divorce statistics in this country, the breakdown of family life and decline in moral values."

"Nick hates solicitors." Sonya gave a wink. "And not just because they are all so filthy rich."

"Nick's friends have to consult the Masserman Marriage Manifesto before contemplating wedlock," Robert added. "I don't recommend it. By the time you're through reading it, you're too old for marriage anyway. He keeps adding clauses, you see, so it's impossible to finish it."

"Then really it's marriage itself that you're against?" Julie asked. She should just change the subject.

"Not at all," he assured her emphatically. And take no notice of this pair. They don't qualify as sane in normal society."

"Oh Nicky!" Sonya's tone had softened and deepened with sincerity and an affection that sounded almost maternal. "When you meet the right person and you finally fall in love, it isn't going to be anything like you're thinking now."

Nicholas smiled magnanimously. "You think so now, but you wait and see. I have no fears on that score, because I know my own mind."

"But can you," Julie interjected softly, "possibly claim to know someone else's mind?"

He was all confidence. "Oh yes! I know I can trust my judgment sufficiently not to make such a mistake." He raised his glass to his lips.

After a brief silence, Sonya turned to Julie. "Why haven't *you* married? You must have been inundated with offers from gorgeous, eligible doctors?"

Julie coughed on her sip of wine and replaced her glass. *Now! Now is the time to disabuse them all of their common misconception and set them right once and for all, possibly proving something to Nicholas into the bargain. People do make mistakes—it's as simple as that.*

But before she could gather in her thoughts sufficiently to reply, Robert announced solemnly, "I believe I can explain that. You see, when I was fifteen I promised to marry Julie...we were, as they say, mutually attracted and, Julie had just lost her front tooth at the time and was going through a very bad patch." Robert shook his head sorrowfully at the sad memory. "Unfortunately, as she was only six-years old, her parents refused their consent. But I vowed to wait for her... for as long as it took the tooth to re-grow and for her to regain her looks and confidence." This explanation, kindled by the wine, produced a fresh bout of laughter and drew a line under the previous topic of conversation.

When Sonya had recovered sufficiently, she began to collect the plates and Julie hastened to help. *Maybe I'll have a quiet word with Sonya in the kitchen. Explain about Simon and my failed marriage.* But girlie-talk about failed relationships was the last thing she wanted right now, so she admired the spacious designer kitchen instead.

"Don't let them tease you." Sonya methodically restacked the dishes Julie had just finished piling haphazardly into the dishwasher. "You have plenty of time ahead of you. Look at plain old me, thirty-one and convinced I was on the shelf, and then suddenly along comes Bob."

Julie spun on her heel, her mouth open to correct the misunderstanding once and for all, but Sonya continued her tirade.

"After all, you can't be more than...let's see...twenty four? Five?"

"Twenty-seven this month," Julie snapped like a child confessing her age to an absent-minded uncle or aunt.

"This month? Really? What date?" Sonya asked, as if the date were genuinely important.

Julie shook her head to try to dispel the otherworldly feeling which engulfed her and bring herself back into the real world again. The gesture failed. Every sentence uttered seemed to send them spinning off at another bizarre tangent.

"The twentieth," she explained.

"So that makes you Taurus—the same as Bob! But only just, of course. You must be on the cusp with Gemini."

"On the what?"

"Oh, don't mind me!" Sonya laughed. "It's just one of my little hobbies—astrology, you know?"

"Surely you don't *believe* in all that?" Julie was all amazement at the thought of anyone being quite so gullible in this day and age.

"Oh yes, of course. I'll show you, if you like. I'll work out your natal chart for you. I promise you won't be disappointed."

"I'm sure I won't," Julie agreed. Did she really want to have a work out of her 'natal chart'? It sounded disturbingly clinical and not at all the sort of thing in which she would be even remotely interested. But Sonya's openness and complete lack of artifice intrigued her. *I bet she's never had a dark secret in her life. And she expects everyone else to be exactly the same. She's completely different to me; to Liz; to just about everyone I've ever known. Except Robert, of course.*

By the time Julie left, she had secured a lunch date with Sonya in town the following day and received Nicholas's assurance of his intention to view the garden on Saturday. She drove home still feeling rather bemused with thoughts of divorces and natal-charts scrambling her brain.

Sonya owned a small shop a little way from the town center called The Mulberry Bush, which sold mainly wood carvings and small furniture items chiefly imported from south-east Asia. There was also a vast array of flamboyantly printed and woven silk and cotton clothing, ethnic jewelry, mostly crafted in silver and semi-precious stones and aromatic oils for all manner of uses.

Sonya had once imported these items herself and distributed them wholesale all over the country as a one-woman enterprise, having made her contacts with the retail world at craft fairs and exhibitions. So great had been the demand for her wares that Sonya had to change warehouses three times in two years. Finally, in exhaustion, she yielded to commercial pressure to sell out to a large chain of arts and crafts importers. She then spent six months scouring different towns in England, looking for the ideal spot to open a shop of her own before settling down to business as a retailer. She was a natural businesswoman however, and immediately foresaw the potential for a trading outlet at Robert's garden center on her first visit there.

Her romance with Robert had grown in conjunction with their business negotiations and one of the small out-buildings had been newly refurbished for a new branch of the business. They planned to open this, in partnership, after their autumn wedding and honeymoon in Indonesia—which of course would also combine a buying trip for new stock. Sonya explained all this as Julie wandered around the shop admiring its treasures.

"You give the impression that everything in your life just slots naturally into place," Julie observed.

"I suppose I do believe in a beautiful scheme," Sonya agreed. "No such thing as coincidence—what is meant to be, will be. But that doesn't make me any the less fascinated by all the mysteries of the universe."

"You seem to have caught a few of those mysteries in this shop." Julie picked up one of a collection of intricate pieces which appeared to imitate reptiles carved from strange pieces of wood resembling tan-coloured fungi.

"Those are my favorites. They're parasites of fruit trees which have to be removed if the host tree is to survive. In these eco-friendly days, this type of carving is particularly popular with the conservationists. Parasite carvers are considered the true artisans of the wood carving hierarchy," Sonya explained. "The skills required to visualize the creature 'inherent' in the parasite and carve it all in one piece are rare."

Over lunch, Julie plied Sonya with questions about her life and work and her diverse new-age interests but carefully refrained from mentioning Nicholas's name. She was determined not to use Sonya as a means of prying into his life, deciding instead to adopt her belief and leave things to 'the beautiful scheme'—if, indeed, there was one.

Sonya's cell phone summoned her back to the shop for an appointment with one of her suppliers just as she was waxing lyrical in her defense of reflexology, one of the alternative forms of therapy in which she found herself lately developing an interest.

"Come to lunch on Sunday so I can demonstrate," she urged, making preparations to leave and rapidly dismissing Julie's protest that it was her turn to offer hospitality. "Oh, we don't stand on ceremony about such things and anyway, we have our non-working Sundays down to a 'T' these days. A very lazy 'T' I should add! Bob and Nicky usually take command of the kitchen—so don't expect anything epicurean, but it leaves me—us—free to put our feet up, literally in this instance, and relax!" Sonya laughed at her pun.

"But what about Nicholas, won't he mind?" Julie allowed herself the enjoyment of saying his name aloud for the first time.

"Nicky? Oh no, it was his idea! Not that I wouldn't have thought of it myself, of course. He just suggested it first, after you left last night. He said if he left it until to tomorrow to ask, it might be too short notice for you. I reckon he's quite taken with you, Julie."

"I think he's very nice, too." she murmured feebly, thinking what an understatement that was.

"Of course you do. Nicky's one of the best." Sonya grew serious. "I don't know how poor Bob would have managed without his support after Linda died. Oh yes, our Nicky is one in a million."

One in a million, Julie mused, but one of what, she wondered.

"That's settled then. Sunday, midday." Sonya squeezed Julie's arm affectionately before they went their separate ways.

Liz raised no objections to the subject of the garden survey and even ventured to agree that landscaping might be quite the thing.

"Garden make-overs seem to be all the rage these days. And it certainly is a bit of a wilderness out there." Liz peered through the breakfast room windows, possibly for the first time in years.

Julie planned her tactics carefully, for once, and before broaching the subject of holding a small dinner party, begged Liz for the loan of her medical school library pass in order to begin her revision of the neurological system. Liz was delighted. "Of course, of course! But if you give Allison a list, she'll get you whatever you need." Allison was Liz's already overworked secretary.

"I'd rather go myself and find my way around," Julie explained. "If you leave your card for me, I can go on Monday. I should have finished nephrology today."

"Are you revising alphabetically?" Liz asked to Julie's great amusement.

Her response to the dinner party was less enthusiastic.

"I expect Mrs B. will cope," she replied in a tone that suggested that Mrs B. was completely incompetent. In fact, Julie had already tentatively suggested the idea to the housekeeper, Mrs Bottomley, who had fallen into raptures of delight that her culinary skills were to receive one of their rare performances and began polishing the silver at once. "But I don't know that I should have much in common with these people, I'm afraid. Robert Ashley," she pondered over the name. "The name sounds vaguely familiar—I wonder if he's a patient?"

"Oh, Liz! You were at school with Robert for years! You were never out of each other's company when you were children," Julie rebuked.

"Really? Oh *that* Robert? Yes, of course we were...but I doubt if he's the same person after all these years."

"Of course he is. How else should we know each other?"

Liz nodded but still looked unconvinced. "Yes, I see. What's Robert been doing all these years?" Liz's attention had already wandered back to the screen of her laptop, which depicted a complex array of numbers and minimal prose. She flicked to the next screen of information.

Julie told her.

"What a coincidence. Didn't you say that the man who is coming here this afternoon is a landscape gardener?"

Julie sighed. "Yes, Liz. He works for Robert."

"Look at this!" Liz exclaimed, alternating between two pages of scatter graph information at a dizzying rate, both of which she was rapidly scanning. "Drat that wretched Henderson! These results are ridiculous. Just look at these readings. These dots mean nothing at all. I suspect he's invented the results!"

Julie listened to the tirade against Dr Henderson, fearing for his future in cardiology. She tried to decipher the charts over Liz's shoulder and allowed Liz to explain to her how the findings failed to agree with the statistical data shown on the charts. She had never seen Liz so angry before.

Fortunately however, she had calmed down considerably by the time Nicholas arrived and even answered the door herself. She evidently saw no need to interrupt Julie's studies and led him out into the garden. Sometime later, Julie raised her tired eyes from the diagram of the renal system she had been studying and trying to memorize, and let them slowly focus on the garden, where Elizabeth and Nicholas appeared to be deep in discussion.

Liz, in her high heels, was almost as tall as Nicholas, so their faces appeared to Julie to be intimately close as they discussed some detail about the right side of the garden. Julie felt a little twinge—not jealousy, surely? What if Liz felt it too, that powerful attraction, animal lust or whatever it was, and after all, why shouldn't she? She was a woman, even if that *was* only secondary to being a doctor, and was still capable of being seduced by an attractive man—or even of seducing him. What a thought! Yet it was easier to imagine Elizabeth seducing a man than being seduced *by* one. Had she ever been seduced? Powerful women like Elizabeth sometimes went in for the more rustic type...'a bit of rough,' Julie had heard it described. Like Lady Chatterley. She was certainly watching Nicholas attentively as she pushed away a stray lock of hair which the spring breeze persisted in teasing out of place. Nicholas, his dark blond hair occasionally sparking gold in the sunlight, was deep in concentration as he sketched onto his tablet pc with a slender stylus, all very professional. She was pleased to see that Robert provided the latest equipment for his staff. Maybe he had made the twenty-first century after all.

Occasionally Nicholas's beautiful blue eyes narrowed in concentration as he paced back and forth and then returned to Liz to discuss some detail or other. Did she have to stand there watching him, like a fox over a chicken? Shame flooded her heart at the thought. He glanced upward to her window. *Was that a smile?* She backed out of his line of vision. She couldn't very well not show herself downstairs now, having been caught spying on him. That would be extremely rude. *Mrs Bottomley will be making coffee. I should go and help.*

Her sister came in just as Julie was putting the finishing touches to the tray. She looked windswept and slightly flustered. "What a charmer he is... and so helpful," she murmured. "Oh good, you've made the coffee—shall I invite him in, or take it out to him, do you think?"

Julie shrugged, affecting disinterest and trying to conceal her growing irritation with Liz for automatically assuming the role of hostess. Lady of the Manor. Lady Chatterley. Leaving Liz to decide, Julie took her own cup into the breakfast room which afforded a clear view over the garden. Nicholas followed Liz across the neglected lawn and into the house. She heard their voices clearly in the kitchen.

"That sounds wonderful...I can hardly wait," Liz crooned.

Hands off, Elizabeth!

"Of course, I can't take on the job myself, but I'll do my best to supervise it at all stages. Subject to Bob's approval, if you and your sister agree we can start in a couple of weeks—the sixteenth or seventeenth, depending on the weather."

"Excellent." Liz spoke for them both, Julie observed. "Do bring your drink through."

Julie jumped up, anxious not to be caught eavesdropping as well as spying, and began to head for the sitting room but Nicholas entered immediately and she was caught like a thief in the act.

"Hello Julie."

"Nicholas!" Julie exclaimed then wanted to kick herself for sounding so surprised. What was wrong with her? She was managing to make a complete fool of herself. She tried to summon her dignity. "I was just going into the sitting room, where there's a nice fire. Please, come through." She pushed open the door and almost toppled the small table on which sat the exotic palm from the nursery. *He's doing this to me...reducing me to ridiculous, clumsy adolescence!*

Nicholas made a remark to Liz about her interest in the species of palm but Liz looked completely blank. She stared at the plant in surprise.

"Oh that? I can't imagine where that thing came from. I expect my housekeeper put it there."

Julie tossed an agonized glance at her sister while Nicholas's eyes sparkled with amusement. "Do sit down both of you," she said. Liz still gazed in puzzlement at the plant.

Julie sat, pursing her lips, determined to provide no more amusement for Nicholas at the expense of her own dignity. Better to let Liz monopolize her new gardener.

"I understand you're a hospital consultant." It was half-question, half-statement, possibly to break the silence.

"Yes. Cardiology is my subject, but I'm afraid it wouldn't interest you," Liz replied sounding, Julie thought with shame, horribly condescending. "It doesn't even interest Julie and she's supposed to be entering the field herself!"

Julie felt her cheeks flame but refused to rise to the bait. This was hardly the time to renew her old argument with Liz, whose expression was particularly sour at this point.

"And do you think," Nicholas continued, "that the new clinic on Nettlesby Road will affect your workload at all?"

"I certainly hope so, since I've helped to found it. I should have twelve beds—if and when it ever opens. The wretched place has been beset with problems from day one." Liz proceeded to outline some of the difficulties and frustrations encountered by the development.

"There's always been a lot of antipathy to privatized medicine in this town," Nicholas agreed.

"That's only because of propaganda and the general public's ignorance of the issues at stake."

"As I understand it, the main funding comes from tobacco money, which the government feels should be channeled into the Health Service—and that's what the general public feel too."

"But we know, and the tobacco giants know, that if the government gets its hands on the money, it will merely subsidize the Health Service budget and the people targeted to benefit will never do so." Liz was riding her favorite hobby-horse.

"Meaning those who can afford private health care?" he asked dryly.

"But that's just the start. Everyone will benefit from the advanced facilities and the research, don't you see? And there will be discretionary beds available. People go on about this country's so-called free health care, but do you know how rapidly it's being eroded?"

Before Nicholas could reply, Mrs Bottomley put her head around the door to summon Liz to the house phone. Julie hadn't heard it ring. She had listened to the debate between Liz and Nicholas with mounting interest and admiration of Nicholas for his grasp of the subject and forthright argument. Anyone prepared to challenge Liz's dogmatic views deserved some respect.

"I can't decide if you're studying law or corporate finance, but take it from me, you'll get nowhere trying to make Liz see any other point of view about her precious clinic," she told him.

"Who said I wanted to? I'd much rather discuss your career in cardiology," he countered with a teasing smile. "Are you afraid of setting yourself in competition with your formidable sister or do affairs of the heart simply hold no interest for you?"

Julie grimaced. "I'll make a pact—I won't quiz you about *your* career if you don't quiz me about *mine*."

He seemed to give the proposition serious consideration before agreeing, then he glanced at his watch and rose to leave. "I have to go. I have a lot of work to do this afternoon." He sounded genuinely regretful. At the door, he paused for a moment, his face so close that she could feel his breath on her cheek.

"I look forward to seeing you tomorrow. I'm so pleased you can make it." And he was gone.

Back in her room, she found it impossible to return to her studies and her curiosity about Nicholas was more fired up than ever. Simple gardener or not, this man was having a very disturbing effect on her and she wondered how she could have been married to Simon for so long and been completely unaware of the disturbing depths of her sexual feelings. She rationalized that these feelings she had for Nicholas must stem from nothing more than sheer physical attraction. How else could they be explained? She knew nothing about him...they would probably have no common interests. She knew precious little about horticulture, although she loved wildflowers.

Even if he were an artist or writer, there might be little common ground between them. Her knowledge of art was limited to the occasional London exhibition, a week in Florence and a long weekend in Paris, which had incorporated only a fleeting tour of The Louvre. As for literature, her reading had been almost entirely restricted to medical text books for years. There had never been time, since entering medical school, nay, even before then, for exploring artistic or literary preferences. She enjoyed music and the theater and cinema whenever time permitted, but could never attend either without a sense of guilt, such a slave to her studies had she become ever since entering medical school.

Julie had never been the sort of person to whom success in exams came easily, unlike Elizabeth, who had distinguished herself in every exam she had ever faced with seemingly minimal effort. Julie had passed through medical school partly on the strength of Elizabeth's reputation, partly thanks to Simon's unstinting help and patience, but chiefly through seriously hard slog. When her fellow-students indulged in the sort of revelry for which students were notorious, Julie crammed feverishly for the next exam or piece of coursework. What others seemed to manage in a few hours, invariably took Julie several weeks.

"I would have been happier stacking shelves at Tesco." She turned to her own bookshelves. On one of these she had stored some of her mother's favorite texts and her finger brushed along the old and worn spines until it came to a slender volume so worn that its title was no longer legible on its vellum spine.

She removed it carefully. It was a collection of Shakespeare's Sonnets and even after all these years, it still fell open on what had almost certainly been her mother's favorite: *Shall I compare thee to a summer's day?* A few penciled annotations in her mother's neat hand littered the margin, too faint to read now, though Julie squinted and screwed up her eyes to try to do so. At the bottom was a brief comment followed by a question mark. She could just make out the single word 'immortality', but nothing else and she read through the sonnet trying to imagine herself into her mother's mind, seeking the same question she had sought all those years ago.

After reading it several times silently, she found herself reading it aloud, very quietly, enjoying the sensuous softness of the iambic rhythm and words as they rolled off her tongue.

> *So long as men can breathe, or eyes can see*
> *So long lives this, and this gives life to thee.*

Or was it 'immortalizing?' But immortalizing what? Julie wondered. Poetry, perhaps? Was that what her mother had questioned? As long as people live and have eyes to read, then the written word lives on...surely that's what Shakespeare was claiming? She frowned, squinting again at the faded lettering. Immortalizing love? Of course it might be that too...keeping the beauty of his love alive by the written word, perhaps?

Julie felt suddenly elated, suddenly very close to her mother's questioning mind. What she needed was to find an expert to show her the key. Could that possibly be Nicholas? she wondered with mounting amusement. Could they have elevated conversations about Shakespeare? She laughed at herself, but all the same, took the book of sonnets to her bed where she lay on top of the soft duvet slowly flicking over the pages, reading lines here and there as they caught her attention and letting the lovely words speak to her heart until she found herself reading and re-reading lines more slowly and carefully. She closed the book suddenly, eyed her laptop with some misgiving and then glanced at her watch. It was almost four o'clock. If she hurried, she might just catch the library before it closed.

CHAPTER THREE

Sunday dawned, bringing convincing, if false, promises of summer with its morning garments and Julie carried her coffee, books and newspapers out to the garden to commune with the flirting day...the garden that was soon, under the watchful ministrations of Nicholas, to be altered beyond recognition. Would he make dramatic, architectural statements with some of those huge, exotic palms or turn it into a cornucopia of flowers?

Julie felt changed since *Discovering Shakespeare*, as she now thought of her sudden journey from literary ignorance into enlightenment and she reveled in the mingled scents and colors of the spring growth, the busy thrum of insects already urgently about their life-work and the manic chatter of the birds frantically making up for time lost by the late arrival of the spring this year. A butterfly fluttered nervously around her head, test-driving its new wings, and for a moment, seemed about to settle on one of her dark curls on which the morning sun bestowed its kisses. Julie threw back her head to enjoy the sensuous warmth of the sun's flirtation.

"You look like the cat with the cream this morning." Elizabeth sounded tired as she entered the garden from the open French windows of the breakfast room, still in her dressing gown and with her hair springing about her narrow face in wild disarray.

"You should do something about your hair, you know. It's such a beautiful color, especially when the sun catches it. With a really good cut it could be stunning." Julie's words caused Liz to halt in her tracks for a moment in surprise as she surveyed her sister carefully, as if checking for further signs of dementia. Evidently finding no clinical corroboration, she let her fingers brush impatiently through her hair, leaving it standing out in every direction and almost, though not quite, smiled.

Julie knew that Elizabeth never gave much thought to her appearance, although she had a congenitally good dress-sense and the money to afford clothes of such superior quality that they could hardly fail to look smart. Nevertheless, when it came to making herself attractive, she was at a complete loss and appeared touched and rather flattered by Julie's sisterly concern.

"Yes, I suppose I should do something with it, but I just never seem to find the time for that sort of thing," she confessed.

"Then I'll search out the best salon and arrange an appointment for you," Julie offered.

"Better check with Allison first, I suppose." Liz peered at the assortment of books beside Julie's seat. She picked up one of them as gingerly as someone newly-cured of arachnophobia might pick up a small spider. *"The Sonnets Simplified."* She sounded amazed. "What can this possibly have to do with the renal system?"

Julie smiled. "Offer a little light relief? I got it from a local book shop—it isn't very insightful, I'm afraid."

The library had been cleaned out of Shakespeare criticisms due, so the librarian informed her, to dwindling demand for what she called 'real books', thanks to the internet and the fact that it was exam season. It was the only time of year the Shakespeare shelves were emptied, presumably by those younger students or their parents who hadn't yet befriended search engines or electronic books. The university had a vast library and the undergraduates and research fellows rarely thought of looking for literary criticisms in the town library, so stocks had never been extensive.

The librarian could not have been more helpful. It was near closing time and the library was virtually empty. She was a great fan of Shakespeare herself, she confessed—loved Stratford, adored The Globe—seen many plays.

"With a name like Juliet—" She scanned the newly completed application form. "I could hazard a guess at your parents' favorite play."

Julie smiled and asked her about the Sonnets.

"I once bought a volume for a man I loved. It seemed so appropriate at the time, but...well, he turned out to be married and somehow I didn't really trust romantic poetry after that. However..." Her fingers danced over the computer keyboard and screen after screen of titles scrolled before their eyes. She scribbled down one or two of the more recent publications, suggesting the local book shops.

Julie managed to find a couple of the titles suggested by the librarian in the town's largest book shop and had spent the evening reading, comparing, considering and typing probing questions into Google in the hope of finding further elucidation. *The Sonnets Simplified* disappointed her, leaving too many questions unanswered. She even felt that she could have written a better analysis herself. Julie now watched her sister rummage through her books, looking no doubt for *Nephrology Simplified* or some equivalent, but passing no comment until she found the little worn anthology.

"Goodness, where did this come from? It was mother's."

"I know. I have quite a few of her books in my room."

"You do? After all these years?" Liz began turning the pages very gently as she let her eyes scan from one sonnet to another. "I remember some of these—they were her favorites—she loved reading them aloud. I never cared for them myself, never understood them, never had the time...oh! Look at this:

> *Shall I compare thee to a summer's day?*
> *Thou art more lovely and more temperate:*

"I remember her reading this to us right here, under this tree. She was nursing you in her arms, yet looking at me, so I never knew who she was talking about, if indeed it was either of us." Liz's face had taken on a dreamy, abstracted expression.

A soft sigh escaped Julie's lips. "I wish I had your memories, Liz. I wish I could remember mother like you do."

Elizabeth, seeming not to hear, continued turning the flimsy pages of the fragile book, in much the same way as her sister had done the previous night, scanning lines picked out seemingly at random and Julie watched her, almost enviously thinking,

So long as men can breathe and eyes can see
So long lives this, and this gives life to thee.

How much better it would have been to have spent one's university years studying beautiful poetry and arguing finer meanings, instead of studying anatomy and learning how to dissect organs.

Julie watched her sister quietly communing with her dead parent through Shakespeare's words and didn't interrupt. She'd expected a morning of quizzing and renewed discussions about her future in medical practice, but somehow the whole world seemed to have changed this morning, turning somersaults and surprising them all. And now, here they were, before ten in the morning and from somewhere Julie could smell the pungent aroma of burning grass as she leant against the crumbly old trunk of the apple tree and let the wispy, fragmented memories of her childhood filter back through time with the smoke from the neighboring bonfire. And through the smoke a flickering memory uncurled and played before her like a very old film, fogged and almost completely drained of color and without sound, yet the words, "Push me, mummy! Make me ride higher!" rang in her ears and she knew the voice was her own and that somewhere this memory had been immortalized on celluloid, a little spot of time encapsulated forever. *So long lives this, and this gives life to thee.*

"Do you recall what happened to all those old films we had?" Julie broke into her sister's nostalgic reverie.

"No, what?" Liz asked as if on cue, like some childhood rehearsal of a comic act.

"Liz! I mean all the old home movies and the projector we used to have."

"Yes, of course! In the loft somewhere, I'm sure. Mrs B. will know..." But Julie had already disappeared in the direction of the house before Liz completed her sentence.

Walking into the incongruously clean and tidy loft was like stepping into a museum for Julie as she confronted the real memorabilia of the Somerville family, not the dredged up memories of someone else's distant reminiscences. She picked her way carefully along an avenue of aging musical instruments, discarded sportswear from lost or won hockey, tennis, lacrosse and riding events, through an arcade of carefully stacked and framed paintings, all individually wrapped in dust covers, and crates of old, discarded toys and a virtual treasure trove of boxes full of relics from Elizabeth and Julie's school days.

It was like entering an ancient dream in those far reaches of the attic room, when she raised the lid of a box and picked up exercise book after exercise book labeled in a painstakingly neat infantile hand *Juliet Somerville*. She pulled out a rolled-up picture from a dark corner and, as she opened it, she felt a downpour of dried paint showering into her lap. At the top, left corner, in neat script—certainly not Julie's—was the title 'My Family' and underneath four shapes, one stage higher on the evolutionary ladder than stick-men, each neatly labeled 'Daddy' 'Mummy' 'Elizabeth' 'Juliet'. She noticed that Daddy, Mummy, Elizabeth and Juliet all appeared to be holding hands. Julie let the picture roll back into its accustomed shape, releasing another shower of paint dust onto her lap. She pulled out an exercise book and opened it at random. *My daddy is a doctor. He is very tall. He sometimes works in the garden on Sunday.* The words meant nothing to Julie and she glanced at the cover of the book. *Miss E. Somerville* had been crossed out and *Eliza Somerville Esq.* written beside it with a date some twenty-five years previously. She smiled and wondered how it had found its way into the wrong box in such a meticulously-kept system.

Juliet is a conscientious worker but tends to be somewhat diffident, she read from one of her old school reports. She remembered those old reports and hated them. She had thought *diffident* meant the same as *different* and had been both frightened and excited until Liz made her look up the word in the dictionary. She put the report back in the box and replaced the lid, aware that her sister had followed her into the attic and was also rummaging through boxes.

"Here they are!" Liz exclaimed from the other side of the long attic room. She was lifting and shaking a very large old hat box. "And look, here's the projector, as well."

Julie turned and hurried after her sister, down to their father's old study where the family had always gathered to watch the old home movies. She pulled down the white screen while Liz darkened the room and Julie waited, fingers poised on the light switch, waiting for Liz's order, "Lights!" and off they went and before their eyes the years rolled away in an instant.

"There you are!"

"Just look at *you!*"

"Oh, how sweet!"

"Look! Look! There's mother!"

"Is it really her?"

"And father, dear old daddy, see how proud he looks?"

"Is that me in that swing?"

"Of course! Who else? You were so frightened at first, but then you just couldn't get enough of it. You wore us all out. 'Higher, higher,' you'd shout. 'Make me ride higher. Over the houses. Higher, higher...' What a shame there's no sound on this batch. Father and I always said we were going to..."

The picture flickered, the film finished and flap, flap, flapped as the spool began to spin faster. Liz caught it and brought it to a halt.

"What, Liz? What did you and father plan to do?" Julie asked.

Elizabeth gazed at the blank white screen, looking immensely sad. "We said we were going to put sound to it one day. We were going to...record an amusing sound strip to run simultaneously...we used to rehearse the things we'd say. We laughed so much. But of course we never got round to it. So long ago. Later, I planned to transfer it all to video...now of course it would be digital...how quickly technology moves on. But there never seemed to be time, then or now. Poor father was always so busy."

Julie sighed again. She wished she had these memories of her own instead of relying, vicariously, on the unsatisfactory and often unimaginative memory of her sister.

"Oh look, here's one when you first started walking..." Liz started the projector again and talked Julie through the events of her early life which had no reality, except in her older sister's mind and the cracked and jumpy celluloid images dancing on the screen before her. A child, quite a pretty little infant, tottering towards the old apple tree, where, hidden in the shadows, strong and loving arms stretched out and raised the delighted little girl aloft until she could almost touch the branches, then reel after reel of the two little girls in their various stages of early development, all seemingly marked by some sort of final celebration under the protective boughs of the apple tree. The later reels showed Lizzie, expert horsewoman, point-to-point champion, while Julie, in the background, held on nervously to a tiny, docile pony.

"Nettlesby point-to-point! Oh I remember that!" Elizabeth exclaimed. "Look! There's Robert and Bully! Do you remember how we quarreled over that name? Such a beautiful chestnut and he gave it that horrible name! We didn't speak for nearly two weeks over that."

Julie eyed her sister in astonishment. Only yesterday, she had been hard-pressed to remember who Robert was and now today she was remembering not only Robert, but her childhood quarrel about his horse's name! What a difference a day makes, indeed.

"And look, there's Eva and her brother Giles Anderson...obnoxious brats! I remember, we were at this birthday party once and that little toad... oh drat!" The screen looked as if a gigantic spider had begun to eat it from the center outwards. "Damn thing was always doing that. We must stop it before it chews up the film!" Liz snapped off the power supply as Julie switched on the lights. "Caught it!" Liz exclaimed triumphantly and, prizing open the side panel she began to gently coax the strip of film back along its tiny teeth-like sprockets. "I'll splice that later. Now, if I remember correctly, I need to hold my finger on this little...yes! Lights out, please." The years once again rolled away and the child, Julie, clapped her hands in glee as the rosette was placed on her sister's mare and there was a party in the garden, under the apple tree, to celebrate the event, and just behind the apple tree but not quite out of sight of the camera, Robert and Liz settled their differences with a clumsy kiss and then the picture fogged and faded again.

"Oh curse it!" Liz cried in exasperation. It's the wretched lamp now. No wonder home movie making had to move on so quickly. People were dropping dead of exhaustion from this archaic system!"

"Excuse me," Mrs Bottomley called from the doorway as Liz busied herself once again with the projector. "Only I was wondering if Julie had changed her mind and would be staying for lunch after all?"

"What?" Julie glanced at her watch in alarm. "Oh, good grief! I had forgotten completely! Thank you so much, Mrs Bottomley. No, I don't need lunch, thanks. What I need is a time machine!" And with a quick apology to Liz, she fled the room.

Forty minutes later, she drew the car to a halt outside Robert's expansive bungalow. He answered the door looking, Julie thought, slightly drunk.

"Ah here she is!" Robert hugged Julie rather more affectionately than was really warranted. "One more drink and then we were about to launch a search party."

"One more drink and he's about to pass out, more like." Sonya gave an airy wave of greeting from a blue sofa on which she reclined in luxurious abandon.

"I'm terribly sorry..." Julie began but Sonya waved away her words.

"Don't apologize. The potatoes won't be burnt for ages yet and we always have burnt potatoes on Sunday, don't we Bob?"

Bob grunted in reply and threw himself down into an armchair in front of a TV the size of a small cinema screen and tuned to some antiques program, with the volume barely audible.

"Come and apologize to me," Nicholas invited from the kitchen doorway. "I'm curious to know why you're so late even if no-one else is."

"Peace offering." Julie held out a bottle of wine as she entered the kitchen.

He scanned her face as he received the bottle from her. "I think you've been crying! Has your sister been bullying you about your career in cardiology?"

Julie smiled and raised herself onto the edge of the pinewood table. "Not at all. I've just been on a treasure hunt...in our loft. That's how I lost track of the time."

"But did you find the treasure?"

Julie nodded. "Reels and reels of old films. Lizzie and me as children—first steps, first day at school, Christmas concert, you know the sort of thing?"

"Indeed. I have my own private collection."

"Liz and I were quite lost in the past and I felt like I was seeing a different person...until the projector gave up the ghost and Mrs B. reminded us about lunch."

"Good for Mrs B."

"But it's a terrible excuse."

"No it isn't—it's the best I've heard today. I can just picture you watching old movies and weeping for your lost innocence. Did you have pig tails?"

"Of course. And masses of freckles."

"White socks?"

She nodded.

"I should like to see them."

"Not likely, I'm afraid. The projector just gave up the ghost," she said.

"Ah the trials and tribulations of Super 8—I take it they were?"

Julie shrugged. "There was an eight in there somewhere. I'll have to check with Liz. We did get a camcorder later on but I expect we recorded over those tapes. Nothing very exciting, though, I'm sure."

"Well don't be so sad. I have about three old projectors—we can have a night of erotica." He moved in front of her perch and placed his arms on her shoulders, clasping his hands together behind her neck. She had to part her knees slightly to allow him access. "Pig-tails, freckles, gymslip..." he whispered in her ear, "it didn't take you long to find my weakness, Julie!"

"Fool!" She laughed. "So tell me how you appear in your old films?"

He gave a mock groan. "Terrible! I wore a brace on my teeth and short pants, the better to show off my fat and dirty knees. Quite the street urchin, in fact."

"Who's got fat knees?" Robert demanded from the doorway. "I've come to check the potatoes."

"They're fine. Go away!" Nicholas ordered over Julie's shoulder. "Can't you see this conversation is x-certificate?"

Convulsed with laughter, Julie let her head fall onto Nicholas's chest as she strove to regain control. She wished very much that he would kiss her or that she could bring herself to kiss him.

"Is Robert a good landlord?" she asked eventually.

"The best. He lets me live here rent-free."

"That *is* the best kind." She felt full of affection for Robert's act of kindness. She leaned back to survey him. "I don't believe you were ever fat."

"Oh, I was! And what's more, my mother was immensely proud of it," he assured her.

"I should like to see your old movies."

"And I should like to see yours."

"Do you think we would have liked each other as children?"

He considered for a moment, before shaking his head. "Probably not. I preferred my friends to have four legs in those days. And the two-legged ones had to be very good at football, which somehow I don't think you were."

Julie bit her lip. Clearly Nicholas was not much of a romantic after all. She thought of a ragamuffin boy with dirty knees— perhaps he had had a hard childhood. "Is your mother still alive?"

He nodded in surprise.

"Tell me, did she ever read you poetry in the garden?"

He glanced at her, she thought, as if she were mad, before replying, "Never. For one thing, very few of my childhood homes ever had gardens and for another...well, let's just say that my mother had other things than poetry on her mind in those days...and in *these* days, come to think of it," he added as a reflective afterthought.

Julie pursed her lips together tightly. The intimate bubble that had been softly expanding around them, cocooning them together in a softly sensuous way, seemed suddenly to pop and she wondered what on earth she was doing sitting here trying to re-invent the two of them in this silly sentimental way to justify her flirtation with a gardener.

She always seemed to manage to say the wrong things to him and to end up feeling ashamed or embarrassed, or both, which was not what she wanted at all. Just now she had humiliated him with her tactlessness, because of her naive desire for some mutually experienced childhood magic. How could she have been so insensitive? No gardens, a mother too pre-occupied to care. A fleeting vision of mother and child moving from one dreary flat to another, keeping one step ahead of the bailiffs, flashed through her mind. She decided that she was not ready for the fun and games the dalliance with this gardener had initially promised and resolved to let it go no further. She was no Lady Chatterley. She doubted she would ever be such a woman of the world.

"I'm sorry," she told him when she could at last find her voice. She tried to slide off the table but found herself trapped by his body. How embarrassing! He was watching her with a puzzled expression on his face but made no move to release her. Instead, he once again locked his hands behind her neck, flexing his arms to gently tilt her face up towards his.

'"O speak again bright angel!' Sorry for what exactly? The lack of gardens or the lack of poetry? Believe me, I was never aware of having been deprived of either until this moment." And before she could open her mouth to protest, his lips found hers and invited them into an altogether more pleasurable occupation. Her resolve melted in an instant at the touch of his softly sensuous mouth, though not before the thought had crossed her mind that the fragment of poetry he had just quoted had, coincidentally, come from Shakespeare.

"If you can imagine your foot from my viewpoint..." Sonya cradled Julie's left heel in her hands. "Then you can imagine that I'm facing a miniature version of your whole body, right?"

Julie nodded doubtfully. She lay on a small sofa in what was obviously Sonya and Robert's large bedroom. Sonya had prepared a foot bath which had been therapy in itself, so silky and aromatic had the water been. She still tingled all over from Nicholas's kiss and wondered how such a simple and natural little thing could have left her entire body feeling so discomposed. Now, as the two men fussed and fretted in the kitchen, stubbornly refusing all offers of help, Julie had soaked her feet in aromatic oils and was about have them massaged by Sonya. It was a sensualist's paradise.

"Now I can make a superficial examination of the main organs of the body by examining your foot."

Julie bit her tongue. The idea was ridiculous. No way, Sonya. Impossible, old girl. A foot massage is bound to be pleasant and bound to make one feel good but under no circumstances can it be diagnostic. Despite her resolve, an involuntary giggle escaped her lips as she suddenly pictured Simon's disapproving face.

"Of course, you're skeptical." Sonya was completely calm. "You orthodox medics always are. Don't worry, I'm not offended. I'm used to it. Now I'm just going to palpate your foot, I'll try not to tickle! Fortunately you're young and in reasonably good shape...some chronic tiredness, that's all. You've been pushing yourself too hard and now your body's telling you to take it easier. You should take notice of its messages, you know. Now this here—

" She exerted a little pressure with her thumb. "This is the whole of the lumbar region and I can feel something here, quite high up—a problem with the kidneys."

"I'm certainly having problems studying them," Julie agreed with a giggle.

"Don't be smart! There's a weakness here and this is a warning..."

Julie sat up suddenly. "You're right! I did have a problem, early last year, about three months after moving to Saudi. I had a renal infection...I felt like I was going to die at the time." In fact, Simon had been so concerned about her that he had booked flights back to London, but then the antibiotics finally kicked in. It had left her incredibly debilitated for several weeks. They had put it down to contaminated water and been much more careful about using bottled water thereafter.

"Well there you are," Sonya said, without sounding complacent. "As you're a doctor, you know what sort of precautions to take in the future. But that seems to be it. A clean bill of health, more or less. You need to relax more, though. You're too uptight."

In a corner of the large room was a free-standing, beautifully carved and painted cabinet which Sonya told Julie had been crafted by a dear friend of hers in Java. When the doors were opened they revealed a veritable apothecary's treasure trove of phials containing aromatic oils and measuring and mixing bowls in glass, wood and marble. Julie was enchanted by the tiniest pestle and mortar she had ever seen. Sonya had already mixed a blend of oils for Julie, but now wanted to create something special and, she said, deeply personal. She measured out droplets of geranium and jasmine and blended them with clary sage and other delightful sounding names, then in went something citrusy and a minute amount of oil of black pepper, which was an aphrodisiac, or so Sonya claimed.

"Are you a witch?" She tried to memorize the ingredients.

Sonya laughed. "I suppose I am in a way. But I promise this won't harm you and I'll write out the recipe if it works."

"If it works?"

"Well it's a whole-body cure, you see. You don't just need to relax and you don't just need to look after your renal status...you need a little bit of soul repair too."

Julie burst into laughter. "Soul repair? My God, you really *are* a witch. Is this going to change my life?"

Sonya smiled, not in the least offended. "I don't know if this will, but *something* will. I've been looking at your birth chart and you are going through a major life-change right now. Now sit down, I want to try this blend out. I think it's going to be very exciting."

An epiphany. Had she read that in one of her sonnets or was it something dredged up from her dim and distant school days? Who was it who had talked about epiphanies in something other than the biblical sense? A poet, certainly. And what was it? Wasn't it something to do with an intensely satisfying experience or a moment of extreme joy? Going through a major life-change? Oh yes! Every day was opening and blossoming and making her look at herself in ways she had never considered before, because she had never really considered herself before. She had always been too busy being Henry Somerville's daughter, or Elizabeth Somerville's sister, Simon Gardiner's wife or struggling to live up to the expectations of consultants and patients. So many vague identities, none of which was really hers.

This day was her epiphany, so acute was her sense of pleasure in it, her sense that everything would radiate outwards from this day, this moment of complete relaxation in the comfort and company of these delightful friends who accepted her on her own merits and expected nothing from her but the simplicity of her presence. No stepping stones to the hierarchy, no introduction to her sister, no quiet words in her husband's ear, no passing of exams, no commitment to the higher causes, etc. Here she could find the space to find herself. In her imagination she saw herself caught in a time-loop, forever re-enacting this day, or one very like it with just these people.

After lunch they sat around in pleasant relaxation, Robert lending half-a-mind to the football on TV, Sonya to repairing an intricate piece of fabric-work and Julie and Nicholas to solving the crossword in one of the Sunday newspapers, but mostly engaged in swapping quiet thoughts and discovering how similar their likes and dislikes were. *If every Sunday from now on doesn't follow this perfect pattern of intimate discovery, then my life will be very thin indeed.* She glanced at Nicholas. *And it's certainly not all to do with Sonya's 'soul-repair'.*

At length, with the crossword completed and both Robert and Sonya deep in wedding discussions, Nicholas suggested in Julie's ear that they might go out for a walk and they slipped away like guilty children.

Outside, Nicholas glanced at the three vehicles in front of the closed doors of the double-fronted garage and, with a shrug, suggested taking Julie's car. Twenty minutes later, they drew to a halt on the edge of Nettlesby wood.

"I want to introduce you to some friends of mine." He took her hand and led the way carefully along leafy avenues, expertly picking out a footpath across the spongy earth until they came upon shy and fragile banks of lilies-of-the-valley cowering beneath their protective, fleshy leaves. "And look over there." A short distance away, velvety-petaled violets, snuggled close to the earth, yielding up their sweet scents so reluctantly. "I didn't realize it would still be so damp," he apologized to her murmured exclamations of pleasure. "What I really want to see is if the columbine has made it yet. It's through here."

Julie watched him deftly pulling away grass and weeds to let the delicate blue heads find the spring sunlight and thought, he is a gardener...no matter what else he might also be...first and foremost, he is a gardener. But he handles these tiny flowers with all the reverence of an artist or even as if he created them himself. She wondered if his earlier deprivation had been responsible for his love of gardens and flowers. She leaned back against a mossy trunk to give him space to work and to watch him admiringly and soon became preoccupied with her own thoughts. When he had finished, he looked around as if to seek her approval and smiled at her.

"When you begin work on our garden, will you promise to be as kind to our old apple tree?" A sudden feeling of sentimentality overwhelmed her.

He smiled down at her. "Given a half-way reasonable defense, I expect I could be persuaded, though as a physician you must know that it's not a healthy tree."

"Isn't it? No, I didn't know that." The thought filled her with alarm.

"Would you like to outline its medical history?"

All of a sudden, the future of the old apple tree became very important to Julie. "It's where all the important things of my early life happened. I took my first steps under its branches and it was where my mother used to love to sit and read. I always knew I would find her there if nowhere else. She made me a swing from one of its branches and I loved that swing. And apart from everything else, it's got something to do with today just feeling so special."

"Say no more! I never harm sacred property," he promised.

Later they collected Julie's box of films and that evening the child Julie and the child Nicholas almost became acquainted with each other, following as they did so closely upon one another's heels across the small screen in Nicholas's room, while their older selves laughed and teased each other. Immortalized on celluloid. How would Shakespeare have reacted to that? Julie wondered. This archaic form of home movies already seems almost as far removed from us in this digital age as Shakespeare does. Does that make film the new poetry? Or was the world just moving forward at a head-spinning pace, impossible to keep up with?

But not for long did she think about Shakespeare or the wonders of cinematography. Their two shadows had grown in significant ways and some twenty or so years later had rediscovered each other in the flesh, celebrating the reunion in a night of lovemaking more intensely sweet and tender than anything Julie could ever before have imagined, much less experienced. And every other thought and concern dissolved into the ether as she gave herself up to the exquisite joys of the sensory feast the physical union of their bodies delivered.

CHAPTER FOUR

Julie dismissed any guilty doubts that nagged at her conscience after that night. If the past was finished for her then it should mean nothing to anyone else. Her attraction to Nicholas was far too strong to be denied and nor could she think of any reason why she should try. She knew that their affair, once begun, must be allowed to run its course. She felt this on an instinctive, almost primitive level rather than a rational one. To deny it would be wholly unnatural and even dangerous for her rather fragile mental state.

According to Sonya, the forces dictating all aspects of her life were in a powerful state of flux, rendering her vulnerable in every respect. Not that she believed any of this nonsense, but it affirmed what she wanted to do. She rounded off her argument by reasoning that if their relationship should develop into anything permanent, which hardly seemed likely given the uncertainty and diversity of their futures, hers in medicine, his in gardening, the arts or whatever else he did to support his existence, then it would be their struggling future together and not their pasts that would occupy all their energies.

As she luxuriated in her bath—to which she had added seven drops of Sonya's aromatic mixture as prescribed—late the following morning, her body tingled with pleasure as her mind relived the ecstasies of the previous night. How had she been married to Simon for so long without experiencing anything remotely parallel to such exhilarating sensations? Sensations so utterly exquisite that even the memory of them seemed physical enough to send delightful ripples through her insides. And she a doctor, who ought to be familiar with the workings of the human body!

Simon's love-making had always been perfunctory and efficient, not insensitive or selfish, but nothing like the slow, sensuous, wonderful experience of the night before, as they'd discovered each other's bodies in languorous ecstasy. But then her own actions and reactions had borne no relation to the way she behaved with Simon. She was a different person with Nicholas. Recreated!

Mrs Bottomley tapped on the door. "There's a nice young man on the phone for you. He says his name is Nicholas and you're expecting his call."

Julie smiled, feeling pleased on two counts. Normally, Mrs Bottomley would have taken a message, not come trudging upstairs seeking her out. Mrs Bottomley considered taking messages to be far more professional. Julie often sat in the kitchen with her during the mornings, chattering away while she drank her coffee, or helping her with some chore, and had become acquainted with Mrs Bottomley's views on life. She now felt as if she had passed a test. That Mrs Bottomley referred to Nicholas as a 'nice young man' pleased her almost as much as his unexpected phone call.

Pulling on a robe over her still sudsy body, Julie took Liz's bedside telephone into her own room and curled up on her bed. "Hello?"

"I just wanted to hear your voice," he told her. "And ask why, in the name of modern technology, haven't you got a mobile phone?" Julie heard an exaggerated sigh and smiled to herself, lips tightly pressed together. People constantly berated her for this. "I called the house but there was no reply. I thought I told you to stay in bed."

"I don't like mobiles and I can't sleep the whole day away like some sloth."

"Pity. I was looking forward to finding you curled up waiting for me."

The image his quiet words created sent a delighted shiver through her. He'd left early that morning, explaining first how to set the house alarm should she go out but exhorting her to rest for the day. "I'm used to functioning on very little sleep," he told her.

She laughed and reminded him that so was she. On her on-call weekends she was lucky indeed to get more than two hours uninterrupted sleep a night.

She'd considered searching his room after he left for clues about him but found the idea distasteful. He trusted her and she was no snoop. She didn't see any tell-tale signs in the room of any artistic occupation—no half-finished canvasses stacked against the wall, or sketchpads or jars of assorted bristles. Nor was there any tangible evidence of literary pursuits. There was a whole wall of shelves but the books were an amazingly haphazard collection of philosophies, biographies and an array of popular fiction and non-fiction. Many of these, of course, could have belonged to Robert.

She'd switched on a computer sitting atop a tidy desk near the window and even opened the start menu, noting the absence of clues on the impossibly tidy screen of the desktop. After tentatively letting the mouse hover over his personal folder and documents, she shut it down again. She didn't want to start poking around looking for personal-sounding files and folders. That was a betrayal of trust.

She'd ask him one day soon to explain himself, but not just yet. She enjoyed her little guessing game. So instead she investigated outside the room and found a cupboard full of clean laundry supplies courtesy of a well-known local laundry service and later amused herself by changing the masculine dark-blue bed linens for a pristine white set. Did Sonya and Robert use the same laundry service? Was that very efficient-looking washing machine in the kitchen ever allowed to live up to its well-advertised reputation? Of course, she quizzed Nicholas about none of these mundane thoughts as she whispered into the telephone that morning.

In the days that followed, Julie forgot about nephrology and was incapable of progressing to neurology. Occasionally she flicked through her anatomy tomes, but her mind wandered off into the realm of daydreams at the first oblique connection it made. Nicholas was no help at all in encouraging a stable study routine for her as he lured her away from her books at every opportunity. She had confessed to him that she wanted nothing more than to give up medicine completely and according to his philosophy, she should therefore not be punishing herself in studying for the forthcoming Membership exam.

"Surely a reluctant doctor is worse than a reluctant teacher—no good to society at all?" he argued. "Besides, it bothers me to think of you doing something that makes you unhappy."

"But we don't all have your luck. Or your diverse talents," she countered.

She wanted to embrace what she thought of as his hippie philosophy but felt she had been born thirty years too late, and then into the wrong family, so she continued to go through the motions, pretending to study but mostly waiting for her next meeting with Nicholas.

She was not long to remain in ignorance about her gardener-lover, however. That would have been impossible given the amount of time they were now spending together. One day he announced his intention of enlisting Julie in a day's truanting to enjoy the summery weather, which had arrived so suddenly and unexpectedly as is often the wont of the British climate at this time of year.

"Spring is such a beautiful time of year. I missed it very much when I was out in Saudi," she told him one day.

"It could snow next week, or turn just as quickly into summer and you'd miss it again," he said, ever the pragmatist.

So they'd spent a day in Yorkshire's renowned national park at one of his favorite haunts that he rarely had time to visit. It was an idyllic day and an intensely romantic night spent at an unobtrusive, though elegant, small country inn. They walked all day, hand in hand, lost in the beauty and clarity of everything around them but mostly lost in each other. It struck her, however, how rarely they were alone. It seemed that every other rambler in the north of England, out celebrating the fine weather, stopped to chat to them about one thing or another.

"Maybe they think we're famous?" Nicholas suggested.

"I certainly *feel* like a celebrity!" Julie was sated with happiness. They say all the world loves a lover—but how can the world *tell*?

They returned reluctantly the next afternoon for Nicholas to attend to some business, which he had been unable to escape. To Julie, study by now merely meant occupying the spaces in between the time spent with Nicholas. She toyed with the pages of text books but saw little of the texts. It felt to her as if she floated in some airy space, removed from all her worries, where she could enjoy the clarity and freshness and breathe deeply without fears or restrictions. She knew it couldn't last and that made it all the more precious and intense. She spent a lot of time soaking in Sonya's aromatic oils and smoothing various lotions and potions into her skin. She sometimes felt as if she were trying to nurse back to life something half dead, something precious and almost forgotten. When she caught herself at it she laughed and shook her head at Sonya and her silly ideas. But when she looked in the mirror, she could see herself as if for the first time, and soon she began to appreciate what she saw.

"'It is the East, and Juliet is the sun!'" Nicholas held her at arm's length and looked at her admiringly when he called for her that evening to take her out for dinner.

Julie laughed. He'd told her that he had been forced by a girlfriend to sit through *Romeo and Juliet* on countless occasions, some fifteen years or more previously—before he realized that the girl, who claimed it was so necessary to her studies, wasn't even studying Shakespeare but was just completely obsessed with the actor playing Romeo.

If the sight of Nicholas in a suit surprised her, the sight of the car he drove left her almost speechless. "Where did you get *this*?" she gaped at the gleaming red Ferrari. Until now they had driven everywhere in her car.

He gave her an enigmatic smile. "Present from a rich admirer. She knows my penchant for beautiful cars."

"Nicholas, I'm being serious."

"So is my penchant for beautiful cars. Come on, get in, I've booked the restaurant for eight."

Julie touched the tan leather upholstery gingerly, savoring the moment before slipping luxuriously into the seat on the passenger side. "I've never been in a Ferrari before." She felt almost reverent as she breathed the earthy leathery smell deep into her lungs.

"Then make the most of it, I don't have it for long," he told her.

So it was only *borrowed*, she thought...from 'a rich admirer', obviously a woman. The memory of Liz in the garden flashed into her mind's eye. Why hadn't she considered this before? A man as attractive as Nicholas must be plagued by the attentions of wealthy women as he tended their gardens. Why should other women feel any differently than Liz, or herself? Could Nicholas be a gigolo, a male escort or toy boy to some vastly wealthy woman...or women? She shuddered at the thought. He didn't seem the type—but then, how would she know that? This sort of thing was becoming more and more common these days as the photographs of ageing actresses parading their gorgeous young lovers across the front pages of the tabloids proved daily. But she wasn't an ageing actress and she wasn't sure if she was *that* broad-minded! This enigma has gone beyond a game and she was going to have to get to the bottom of the puzzle very soon.

However, it was difficult to find ways to question him on the subject in order to elicit the truth, and he seemed disinclined to volunteer much information. *It's not the sort of thing I can just blurt out. Not now. But how much longer can I let this go on? And what rights do I have to quiz him about his life in this way? After all, how much different are my motives to those of the other women?*

It was a small consolation to think that at least an out-of-work junior doctor could not be expected to buy such fantastic love-tokens as classic cars. But what would this woman think if she knew Nicholas was entertaining another woman in her car? She suppressed another little shudder. *Who cares? I have my own good time to think about.*

Nevertheless she continued to feel uneasy, but at least now, she need not be so concerned about his finances. She'd suffered pangs of guilt over his insistence on paying for the inn last night, which included dinner. To appease her conscience, she was determined to make sure she picked up the bill this evening. She'd wanted to offer him money, but was too embarrassed to do so.

The restaurant was French and Julie could only guess how expensive because her menu had no prices on it. Such antediluvian assumptions! But her attention was soon diverted in trying to make sense of the conversation, in fluent and rapid French, between Nicholas and the Maitre d'.

"Do you come here often?" A bit of an inane question considering the obvious familiarity between the two! When she caught Nicholas's eye, they burst into simultaneous laughter. "Oh dear, I must enroll on a course in small talk." She dabbed at her eye with her napkin. "Where did you learn to speak French like that? You speak it like a native."

"I just picked it up. I spent quite a lot of time in France as a child. I never really saw the advantage at the time, but I do now. Do you speak any?"

Julie shook her head. Compared to him, her stuttering schoolgirl French was non-existent. She'd had no real head for languages and when it was no longer obligatory, had dropped it to focus on more useful subjects. "I suppose you come here with your...um...admirer? She has good taste." *Feeble!* Why did I *say* that?

Nicholas smiled modestly. He actually looked flattered! "I like to think so. The food here is fabulous. The trouble is I never get the chance to experiment. It's always decided for me."

Julie's heart sank. *We obviously have more in common than I first thought. People always seem to want to decide about my life for me, too.*

She had unquestioningly followed in her father and sister's footsteps without ever really consulting her own feelings. It was expected that she would go into medicine—expected by everyone, unquestioned by herself. And then when she met Simon, she had unquestioningly let him take over the management of her life. Was Nicholas really so like her? Someone who had allowed others to dictate his life for him? Surely not!

"Surely *you* could refuse?" She wanted his strength to compensate for her weakness.

He laughed. "As if! Gervaise would probably commit suicide. You wait and see. You may think you've ordered your own meal, but what you'll *get* is entirely up to him!"

When the food arrived, Julie admired its truly stunning presentation.

"This looks truly amazing—a real work of art. Are you *sure* we're meant to eat it? Perhaps we should hang it on the wall and just sit and admire it?" She thought it would probably take a junior doctor's monthly salary check to pay for this meal.

Nicholas laughed. "But if you don't desecrate the work of art, you'll simply devastate the chef!"

Speaking of art, he told her that he had heard from a friend about an antique bronze fountain which would be perfect for the garden, as Liz had expressed a particular desire for a water feature. He wanted to establish whether Julie would like it before mentioning it to Liz and the subject changed to discussions about the auction, then the garden, then...

After that Julie did not have to wait much longer to solve the mystery about Nicholas and all was revealed at last when she arrived at Robert's house the following evening. She found

Nicholas sitting with Robert and Sonya and discussing the merits of various properties of which Nicholas had been sent details and was trying to draw up a potential short list. He explained that he had been house-hunting half-heartedly ever since Robert and Sonya had first talked of marriage, but was now determined to search for a new home in earnest in order to ensure his vacation from Robert's house by the time of the wedding. There were five houses under consideration, the details of which he handed to Julie for perusal. She glanced through the folder of glossy papers and photographs from real estate agents, at first briefly and then more carefully. Of the five houses, the smallest was Oak Cottage with six rooms and just over half-an-acre of land.

"That's only in there because of the tree," Nicholas explained. The tree was a two-hundred-year old oak in the garden. "Brackenbury House sounds more promising," he went on, peering over Julie's shoulder. "The grounds back onto Nettlesby Wood so it would be like a country park!"

With its acre and a half and twelve rooms, it virtually *is* a country park, Julie thought. He has to be crazy! He's so obsessed with large gardens that he's lost his marbles! Surely his 'sugar-mummy' couldn't be setting him up in a house as well?

Sonya gave a tactful little cough. "I'm not sure that I should want to live at Brackenbury House. In the first place, it's so isolated and in the second it looks like an old fort—the windows are horribly pokey."

"It's meant to look like an old fort." Robert looked up from his laptop on which he had been rapidly stabbing out customer email responses with two fingers. "That's what its name means. It's an Anglo-Saxon name."

"Well I think the cottage is much cozier, except I wouldn't want the responsibility of that old tree." Sonya was busy applying an intricate stencil in acrylic paints to a small, painted wooden cabinet. It demanded great concentration and her eyes rarely left the Celtic-looking design when she spoke.

They're all at it, Julie thought. They're barking mad! Why are they humoring him? Is this some sort of game they play?

Glebelands was another mansion with a garden the National Trust could take over and open to the public. Nicholas liked the idea of the stream running through the grounds.

"Dangerous for children." Sonya stepped back to survey her artistry.

Children? *What children?* Julie thought wildly. Does Nicholas have children? Surely not, when he's obviously still such a child himself!

"Whose children are you thinking of?" Robert chuckled.

I must get out of here, Julie thought. *I've walked into a madhouse.* She turned to Nicholas and smiled at him uncertainly. "They all sound lovely—why don't you buy them all?" she tried to joke. "And every time you pass 'Go' you can collect two-hundred pounds to pay the rent."

"What?" Nicholas asked, his mind clearly preoccupied with the papers she had relinquished. "Damn! I've left out The Cedars! It must be in my room." He looked at her as if only just realizing she had spoken. "What did you say?"

She shook her head as he rose to leave the room. The moment the door closed, Julie jumped to her feet and confronted Robert, all the agitation she felt showing on her face.

"What *is* this game?" she demanded.

Robert and Sonya glanced at each other questioningly before turning blank faces to Julie.

"Why are you *doing* this? It's so childish! He's really sent off for details of all these properties and you're playing this silly game with him...this is madness. It's *immoral!*"

"What is?" Robert was clearly baffled, his hand poised over his keyboard. "Is it wrong for us to give our opinions when asked? Isn't that what friends are for?"

Julie again searched their faces imploringly and then glanced down at the wad of papers Nicholas had left on the sofa. Her head began to spin. Could they really all be serious and she missed some essential clue? Could Nicholas really afford to buy one of these houses?

She faced Robert once again. "Who *is* Nicholas? I mean apart from being your friend and your lodger and employee. Who *is* he?"

Robert stared at Julie in astonishment as some degree of understanding began to flicker across his face. Then he began to laugh. "My employee?" he repeated, clearly beginning to enjoy the joke enormously. "You think Nick works for me?"

"Yes! He told me he did. Well, part-time anyway—landscape gardening?"

"Nicky told you *that*?" Sonya gasped.

Julie thought furiously for a moment. "Yes! Of course he did." She felt slightly less certain now.

"And you really don't know who he is?" Sonya sounded genuinely concerned and dropped her brush into a cup of water as Robert convulsed in a fresh paroxysm of merriment.

"Then perhaps you'd better ask Nick!" Robert spluttered as Nicholas appeared at the doorway.

"Ask me what?" Nicholas quizzed.

"What stories have you been telling our Julie?" his friend accused, rather than asked.

Nicholas looked at Julie blankly and, as if registering her agitation and dismay, took a step towards her. She retreated, involuntarily.

"You told Julie you worked for Robert as a *gardener!* She doesn't know who you are. What a rotten trick to play on her!" Sonya accused. Julie noticed she had a smudge of green paint on the side of her nose, which made her look faintly comical and detracted from the severity of her remonstration.

"I'll tell you one thing, Nick," Robert chuckled. "At least it shows our Julie's not after you for your money! She was worrying about how you could possibly afford the mortgage!" Then he turned to Julie and asked with feigned innocence, "Do gardeners in Saudi drive around in Ferraris, Julie?"

Julie felt herself color deeply. She could only speak in a whisper. "You said the car wasn't yours."

He frowned and shook his head. "No, I didn't." Realization suddenly dawned. "Oh! I said it wasn't mine for much *longer*. I've been plagued for months by this Japanese chap—a business associate—who wants to buy it. I've ordered a Lamborghini." He said it as most people might say, "I've ordered a pizza!"

"But...what about your *rich admirer*?" She could barely manage to articulate the words.

"Julie, I was *teasing* you! The car was a present from my mother—she's my 'rich admirer'." He smiled and again took a step closer as she lifted her face and looked at him incredulously. "What did you *think* I meant?"

"But you said your mother...I thought your mother..." She stopped and raised her hand to her face, unwilling to go any further. She had made so many mistakes that she felt she needed to think very carefully before accusing him of anything else.

"Quite apart from the lies he's been telling you, Julie," Robert cut into her bewildered thoughts, "surely you've heard of Masserman Enterprises? You must have made the connection?"

Julie looked blankly from the seated Robert to the standing Nicholas. "What's Masserman Enterprises?"

Nicholas bit his lip to prevent the smile that threatened to break out while Robert released a loud guffaw.

"Kitchen, Roberto!" Sonya ordered with commendable force. "Enough of your *Men Behaving Badly* act! I need your help with something. *Now*!"

Robert rose obediently, thrusting his laptop into Julie's hands as he passed. "You're looking right at it," he told her in parting. "Masserman Enterprises own half this town. You really must walk around with your eyes closed, Julie. Hold onto this girl, Nick. I told you she was priceless!"

Julie glanced at the screen which was now displaying the impressive-looking welcome page of 'Masserman Enterprises' with a photograph of Nicholas smiling out at her from behind a desk which could house a small village. She gazed at this for a moment before snapping the laptop closed and spinning on her heels to faced Nicholas squarely. "Let's just recap, shall we? Am I right in understanding that you are seriously rich?"

He shrugged noncommittally, relieving her of the computer. "Well, I'm...fairly comfortable."

"And your mother is probably even richer?"

"Indisputably." He nodded solemnly as he deposited the computer onto a nearby table.

"And you're not a poor gardener working for Robert?"

"Now that's not *entirely* my fault," he protested. "You should have told me you were coming to dinner *before* you offered me a job doing your garden." His expression betrayed his guilt. "If I'd realized I was going to see you again anyway, I wouldn't have had to go along with the act. It was too good an opportunity to miss! But I thought your mistake was delightful. I *want* to do your garden, Julie. I find gardening very therapeutic. Sometimes I wish I *were* a full-time gardener."

"How come you never had a garden as a child?"

"I told you, we were never in one place long enough—we lived in apartments in New York and on the Riviera and always stayed in hotels when we were in London or Paris—when I wasn't away at school that is. And what a concrete jungle *that* was!"

"And I thought your mother was heartless for not reading poetry to you." She could feel her face flaming with embarrassment at her stupid mistake.

"Oh she *was*! And I intend to tell her so the next time I speak to her."

"I feel like such a *fool*!"

"I honestly didn't mean to deceive you. It's my fault for vainly assuming that you'd soon realize who I was. And I really thought you'd worked it out by the time I came to your house. Otherwise...why didn't you simply *ask*?"

"To tell you truth, I still haven't worked it out. Does your company *really* own half this town?"

He laughed. "Of course not. That's just Bob exaggerating as usual. And don't forget, it was *you* who made the pact not to discuss our careers. That's why I assumed you knew about mine. I thought *you* were the mysterious one."

She smiled and shook her head, more at herself than in answer. It seemed they had both been guilty of leaping to wrong conclusions about each other. "But what exactly *is* your company?

"Property development, corporate financing, that sort of stuff— probably would interest you about as much as cardiology! Come to my office and I'll give you a grand tour if you're really interested. It's in Longchamp Square."

Julie wrinkled her nose thoughtfully. Longchamp Square was not one of her usual haunts. "But the only places in Longchamp Square are the Town Hall, The Court Hotel and that great ugly glass office block."

"That ugly glass office block is Masserman Enterprises." He sounded rueful, even apologetic. "But I accept no responsibility for the architecture. That's another of my mother's mistakes. At least you've *noticed* it."

Later that night, he asked, "Did you really think I was a poor, struggling gardener?"

"Well…with a few other talents on the side, of course," she teased.

"What kind of talents?" He showered her face with kisses.

"Artistic ones, apart from the obvious—you know, the ones you just demonstrated."

"And it didn't bother you? Making love to a simple gardener?" His lips moved down to her neck, stopping just below her ear, which he kissed and nibbled gently.

"Why should it? It didn't bother Lady Chatterley, did it?" She wriggled in pleasurable anticipation.

"Lady Chatterley did it with the game keeper," he corrected. "Not the gardener." Then another thought struck him. "You thought I was some rich old woman's toy boy! What does that make *you*?"

"Infatuated. Now just shut up and do that again."

"Not until you explain yourself." He moved in towards her anyway.

"Shh... How can I concentrate with all this chatter? Can't you see I'm studying?"

"Studying what? Evasion?"

"No, anatomy. Now no more talking, just let me know what you think of this." And she turned her attention to demonstrating that she, too, had hidden talents to share.

"Masserman Enterprises?" Mrs Bottomley repeated, averting her eyes for a moment from the two kinds of chocolate she was slowly melting in identical double saucepans. "I should certainly hope so! I was at the opening of the new shopping mall, you know. I actually saw the duchess in person. In fact, I was so close to her, I could nearly reach out and touch her." She went back to gently prodding the melting chocolate as she eyed the strawberries for the fifteenth time with no less suspicion than the first. "Are you sure those strawberries haven't been genetically modified? They're enormous."

"That's because they come from California. They make everything bigger over there," Julie explained not for the first time, but with unflagging good humor.

"Yes but will they *taste* the same? I always think of strawberries as being *English*, not *American*. And up here, they're not normally at their best until June or even July."

"Do try them, Mrs Bottomley and see what you think. Anyway they're really only meant for decoration."

"You've brought strawberries from America for *decoration*?" Mrs Bottomley shook her head as she contemplated the offending fruits solemnly. "Are you sure you won't let me make one of my lemon tarts? Everyone says they're as light as air—or I could do my glazed apple—always very popular, especially with the men."

Julie laughed. "Of course you can do your lemon tart...I was just trying to save you some work when you've done so much. You said the photos with the little shortcakes and meringues looked very nice in the book."

"Oh, in the *book*." She gave a meaningful nod. "But they're all artists' pictures, aren't they? Dipping strawberries in chocolate and adding a couple of little macaroons isn't exactly making a pudding, is it? I mean, those plates looked very empty."

"Let's do the lemon tart in a moment. First, I want you tell me about Masserman Enterprises."

"Oh, yes! Well, you see Angela—that's my friend, Mrs Fenwick—used to be Taylor before she married poor Andrew—worked in the Town Hall and was a good friend of the Mayor's secretary. I think this chocolate's ready now. You have to be very careful with this type, you know. I'll just move them off the heat for now."

Julie glanced at the bowls of melted chocolate, one dark, one white, and then back at Mrs Bottomley. She was completely lost. "The Mayor's secretary?"

"Yes, of course. You see, it was on account of him we had such good places. That's how I got so close to the duchess. Angela bought this beautiful suit in Marmadukes. Linen, it was. Well she needed smart things, working at the Town Hall. And do you know it had the tiniest mark on the hem—you'd need a magnifying glass to see it and I said, 'Oh that will come off with a dab of that new stain remover you can use on anything,' but she showed it to the assistant and got £30 knocked off the price. Can you believe it?"

Julie shook her head and glanced around her for signs that Mrs B. might have been drinking. The conversation was becoming very hard work.

"Of course, it was them that made it possible." She seized one of the bowls of solidifying chocolate and thrust it at Julie accusingly.

"Who?" Julie asked faintly.

"Massermans, of course. Well, I say Massermans, but I understand there's only one of them running the organization now. And him hardly more than a boy. He can't be more than thirty. Not married yet either and very good looking, I hear. A bit of a playboy, though. Drives around in those really expensive sports cars."

"But what has he got to do with the shopping mall?" Julie was excited now she seemed to be getting closer to the mark.

"Well his firm started it, didn't they? Financed it too, or most of it, Angela said. The original developers ran into all sorts of problems, and the council was under such pressure. They had no choice but to call in the trouble-shooters—that's what people round here call Masserman Enterprises. But it's a lovely place to shop and it has these beautiful little coffee gardens. Just like real gardens they are."

I'll bet they are, Julie thought, especially if Nicholas had anything to do with the design features. Gardens in shopping malls—surely that was an innovation? She had seen the new shopping complex on her forays to the town center, but had avoided it assiduously. Seen one, seen them all—that had been her motto. She found such centers claustrophobic and exhausting as well as invariably predictable. In her experience, they were all cloned from the same prototype and always had the same shops, as only the larger chains could afford the rates. She much preferred to explore the little side streets around the outskirts of the town where interesting little shops like Sonya's lurked. However, she could hardly wait for her next expedition to the town center to visit one of Nicholas's coffee gardens.

The dinner Julie and Mrs Bottomley worked painstakingly yet companionably to prepare was hugely successful. Julie had urged Mrs B. to join them, which gratified the good lady's vanity enormously, but she refused the invitation and, leaving step-by-step instructions about the serving of the food, went out to visit her friend Angela, no doubt to reminisce about the time they saw the duchess.

Elizabeth managed to forget about the evening completely, so engrossed was she in the vagaries of Dr Henderson—whose future in medicine was still very much in the balance—and in rectifying and clarifying important research findings in order to prepare the paperwork for her forthcoming spate of lecture tours and conferences both national and international. She arrived as the evening was drawing to a pleasant and relaxed close and, despite her tiredness, brought a second wind to the small party at the rediscovery of her childhood friend. She seemed to slip almost instantly into a comic double act, for the entertainment and pleasure of them all.

Watching them together, Julie wondered whether the pair might not have made a good partnership had their paths not forked so radically in their late teenage years, but then she felt a stab of disloyalty to Sonya, who was so magnanimous in her love for Robert that she was genuinely delighted in his pleasure at this old friends' reunion.

I'd rather be like Sonya than Liz, Julie thought as she watched the cabaret being enacted between her sister and Robert. Sonya knows herself. Liz hasn't even begun to discover herself yet and she probably never will, so obsessed is she in following in father's footsteps and living up to the image he pioneered for his family. Poor Liz.

"You look very pensive," Nicholas whispered in her ear.

When she was sure no-one was looking, she let her lips flutter lightly against his face. "I was thinking about how much I want to give up medicine," she said under her breath.

"What, not specialize in cardiology ever?"

She shook her head.

"That was never my plan anyway. It was all in Liz's mind."

"Then tell her. Why are you so afraid of her?"

The question surprised her. Was she really afraid of Liz? Surely not! Watching her now, she actually felt vaguely sorry for her. Yet all her life, she had submitted to Liz. And all her life, she had seen other people do the same. Even Robert, as a child, had given in to Liz's wishes more often than he held out against them. After all, he had changed his horse's name from Bully to Bonnie at her insistence.

CHAPTER FIVE

The day Nicholas had chosen to start the garden transformation happened to be Robert's birthday and Sonya planned to organize a party to celebrate the event. As the seventeenth fell on a Wednesday, the party was deferred to the following Saturday, which coincidentally and to Sonya's profound delight, happened also to be Julie's birthday, thus doubling the need for celebration.

During the preceding week, Julie found herself drawn into clandestine meetings to plot and scheme over suitable surprise gifts for Robert, and Sonya attacked the event with as much energy and enthusiasm as a doting parent might put into the first proper party of his or her firstborn. Should the party have a theme, or perhaps be fancy dress? Should they risk a marquee in the garden, or decorate the house? And of course, there was the paramount question of the cake.

During the same period, Nicholas managed to view all five houses on his list and at his request Julie had accompanied him to three of the viewings. A tree surgeon had examined the oak, an architect the 'fort' and a surveyor was exploring the source and history of the stream.

Julie was all curiosity about the houses, but was worried at first about appearing too eager to accompany Nicholas. After all, their relationship was in its infancy and to go viewing houses with him might seem to suggest she was pushing it to a more mature level than Nicholas intended—or than would be considered appropriate in the time that had elapsed. She didn't want him to think her too eager. Besides which, their opinions were so similar that she genuinely felt she would be able to contribute little objectivity. For this reason, she tactfully suggested that Sonya might make a better viewing companion, but Nicholas only laughed.

"I've no doubt she'll involve herself soon enough, but I want to get the feel of the places myself first before I have to think about energy lines and missing spaces and whether the staircases will need to be moved!"

Julie smiled, secretly delighted. Sonya was a firm believer in the principles of Feng Shui and had already poured over her charts and maps to ascertain the most propitious timing and best directions for Nicholas to move. She had also disqualified Glebelands, on the grounds that it lay in the wrong direction and Oak Cottage, after glancing at the plans and realizing that the immense oak was in a threatening position and sending 'secret arrows' towards the house.

"That cottage has probably had one occupier after another and all will have moved away due to relationship break-ups or ill-health, you mark my words," she lectured solemnly.

Julie thought Glebelands was too austere, though she didn't share her thoughts with Nicholas. The house was large and uninviting and there was a harshness to the way the natural light entered several of the rooms, for which Julie could not account, though Sonya doubtless would. The grounds were large and boringly subdued except for the corner where the stream cut across. She could tell Nicholas was unimpressed.

At the second house, they were met by a rather unctuous estate agent who almost danced a jig at the sight of the Ferrari and who kept referring to Julie as Nicholas's 'good lady,' which made her cringe but afforded Nicholas immense amusement.

"That horrible man thinks we're married," Julie whispered as they followed the loquacious agent up the stairs.

"No he doesn't," Nicholas teased. "He's just trying to flatter you into exerting your feminine wiles over me."

The 'place' was a sensible five-bedroom detached house that had been well lived in and had quite an interesting character. It was convenient for the town center whilst maintaining something of a rural air because of the open space on one side and the village green at the front. The garden was surprisingly large and well laid-out with some unusual architectural features and mature plantings. Julie thought it would make a very comfortable family house. Nicholas was reluctantly impressed by it, she could tell. But he was not *in love* with it. It was a good house, but not a perfect one.

Another agent showed them The Cedars. This time it was a woman who introduced herself as Annabel Campbell-Turner. She was tall, sleek and very attractive, if in an overly groomed way, with blonde hair and a meticulously made-up face, which made her look more like a glamour model than an estate agent. She exuded sex-appeal and from her first words, projected it all at Nicholas. If she formed any opinion about Julie's relationship with him, she kept it to herself. She knew who Nicholas was and claimed a former though brief acquaintance with him, which Nicholas was at a loss to recall.

"Don't you remember the Barrington-Jones's party last August?" Annabel Campbell-Turner prompted. "You were with—" here a quick glance at Julie and a meaningfully lowered voice— "Clarissa at the time and she introduced us."

Nicholas made polite noises. Annabel linked his arm and led him towards the house, pausing at the front door to turn and beckon Julie to follow. "You are going to positively adore this place, my dears."

They did. And Julie was sure that she, for one, would have adored it even more without Annabel's rapacious flirting.

The house was light and clean and airy, but with none of the harsh brightness of Glebelands. Julie was sure that the two tall trees, after which the house received its name, must surely be in the best position possible for the house, whilst at the far end of the mature garden she could see a promising cluster of exotica, including a dramatic black stemmed bamboo and something resembling a banana. Already the garden was a riot of color and shape from well-placed shrubs and flowering plants that looked as if each had been individually chosen to present a feast to the eyes the entire year round.

"This garden has taken a great deal of careful thought and planning over a long time." Nicholas stood close behind Julie and murmured in her ear as they gazed out through one of the tall windows. His lips were tantalizingly close and she allowed herself to relax for the briefest moment against him and enjoy the sensuous luxury of his nearness, which always caused her flesh to tingle with pleasure.

"It's a real work of art. Not short of TLC," sang out Annabel. "Not like some of *us*, eh?"

Julie turned her head towards Nicholas. "Don't you wonder why the owners want to sell?" she whispered, but not quietly enough for Annabel's sharp ears.

"Oh, I can tell you all about *that*. Their reasons are completely genuine and benign. But you haven't seen upstairs yet, Nicholas. You must look at the master bedroom. It's to die for." She seized his hand and pulled him away from the window. He threw a quick grimace at Julie followed by an almost imploring look.

Julie continued to wander around downstairs for a while, relieved to be away from the awesome Annabel. The house had been stripped of its furniture downstairs and Julie presumed there was none upstairs, least of all a master bed in the 'to die for' master bedroom. There were six rooms downstairs, as well as a modern spacious kitchen with a smaller utility room. She tried to guess how Nicholas might use them all as she wandered from room to room, her heels clip-clopping along floorboards sealed and polished to silken perfection and glowing warmly in the sunlight filtering in through the tall windows. I could be so very happy here, she thought. With Nicholas.

When she eventually went upstairs Annabel appeared to be trying to wrap her slender body around Nicholas, who was beginning to grow irritable and after a cursory glance at the upstairs rooms, said he had seen enough.

Annabel appeared undaunted about the loss of a sale, but was clearly dismayed by the prospective loss of Nicholas. "Take my card. Call me any time, I mean *any* time. That's my office number, my mobile and... I don't ordinarily give this one...my home number." She scribbled a row of numbers on the back of the card. "And this is my e-mail, or you can find me on Facebook and the like. Or perhaps you'd prefer if I called you?"

Julie went to wait beside the car so she could not hear Nicholas's reply. She watched him see Annabel into her own car, a sporty Mercedes, red like the Ferrari, about which he paused to make a few appreciative comments.

At least they have one passion in common, she thought, expensive red cars. *I wonder if he's arranging to test-drive hers?* As Annabel drove off spewing gravel behind her, Nicholas walked towards his own car and eyed Julie across its roof in silence for a moment. Then he looked back towards the house.

"What did you think of it?" He still sounded irritable.

"The house, the car, or the man-eater?"

He released a small explosion of grim laughter, which seemed also to release the tension. "Oh, you did notice? I wondered if you were being tactfully aloof or simply didn't care."

She came around the car to face him and spoke severely. "Nicholas, you are a seriously attractive, seriously wealthy and, even more astonishingly, a seriously eligible man. Surely the last credential alone means you must have become an expert in dealing with women like *that* by now? You didn't *really* think I was going to scratch her eyes out for you, now did you?"

"Tell me you wanted to, though," he urged, putting his arms on her shoulders and cupping his hands behind her neck in the now familiar gesture, all irritation vanished from his voice.

"Tell me you didn't know she would be meeting you here!" she challenged.

"She gave me a name. I had no idea who she was. If only women like that realized what a complete turn-off they are."

"I thought she was very attractive."

"True and she had a very attractive car. I expect she has admirers coming out of the woodwork, but she's not my type." He delivered the last words slowly and with emphasis.

"What about the house?"

Nicholas deposited a kiss on the top of her head and gazed thoughtfully back at the house for a moment. "Now, *that* just might be. I think I'll contact the agents again—see if I can bribe them into letting me have the keys to look at it again next week sometime, without an agent breathing down my neck."

On the morning of the seventeenth, Nicholas arrived with three young men from the garden center and spent the better part of the morning in instruction and discussion with them. On the days following, he would arrive at various hours of the day to make brief inspections and talk over details with the gardeners. The weather, during that week, had turned unusually cold again and Julie and Mrs Bottomley fretted over the three industrious boys working frequently without jackets. Mrs Bottomley cosseted them with a steady stream of hot drinks and snacks 'to keep up their strength' and during one of their many refreshment breaks, Nicholas arrived and ordered Julie, with mock severity, to stop pampering them. She suggested that they postpone the work until the cold spell passed, but Nicholas only laughed.

"They're used to it—and they also recognize a soft-touch when they see it. Apart from which, if we postpone the work now, it will be the summer before they can fit it in, and I don't want you to be deprived of your garden during the summer months. So no postponing, and if you attempt to undermine my authority again, you'll have *me* to answer to." His voice was stern, but as the threat was sealed by a lingering kiss, its severity was nullified. They were standing beneath the apple tree, which creaked sorrowfully under a sudden blast of wind. They both looked up into its branches simultaneously.

"Rough winds do shake the darling buds of May. And summer's lease hath all too short a date;" she quoted.

"I'm afraid this tree's lease may well be *very* short if we don't do something about it soon," Nicholas informed her gently. "You can see how few 'darling buds' it has. I've had Jackson's report and he claims it's not really worth the cost of treating it."

"Oh no!" The expression on her face matched the sadness in her voice.

He kissed her again and smiled. "But I've told him to do what he can. We're not giving up on this old patient yet," he promised.

And she thanked him with a profusion of kisses, which he accepted as his due.

By Saturday the weather had changed again and Julie looked out of her bedroom window onto a golden morning. The garden by now was unrecognizable and looking a complete shambles. It was impossible to imagine the transformation that was about to take place before her eyes and she sorted through the digital images she and Nicholas had taken the previous week in order to make before-and-after comparisons. Nicholas had arrived one afternoon with his camera to find Julie already clicking away in garden. Both had shared the same thought, that no matter how good the new garden was, the old one would always hold special memories. It was just one of those harmonious coincidences they shared, which demonstrated how closely in tune they were.

But some coincidences are not so fortuitous. Some, indeed, are catastrophic. It was no real coincidence that Simon telephoned that afternoon—he had never forgotten Julie's birthday before, so it seemed unlikely that he would now.

"It's good to hear your voice, Jules. *Happy birthday.* How's everything with you?"

"It's nice of you to remember. Thank you, Simon. Everything is fine, what about you?"

"You're the birthday girl, we should talk about you. What have you been doing and what's it like being back home with Lizzie? No regrets?"

She smiled. He meant about going to live with Elizabeth, not about leaving him. Simon and Liz had never been the best of friends, though they tolerated each other with a commendable degree of civility. "I hardly see her. She's always at the hospital."

"Ah yes, the busy consultant. Is she cracking the whip over your Membership exam?"

"To be sure. I'm planning to have a stab at it in November." Julie felt horribly guilty at the glib lie. She had barely thought about the exam in the last few weeks. "How have things been in Riyadh? How's Arnold?" Arnold Jefferson ran Riyadh's busiest clinic, where Julie had worked alongside Simon.

"He's fine. Sends you his love. I've been thinking about the house, Jules." He meant their house, their marital home in London, which now stood empty.

"*I* don't want it, Simon. I don't want to live there. Do you think *you* ever will?"

There was a long pause before he answered. "No. I doubt it. I think we should sell it. Do you think you could look into it for us?"

"Of course I will, Simon. Whatever you want." Julie turned suddenly, as people so often do when they become aware of another person's eyes on them. She was just in time to witness Nicholas spinning on his heels and walking away. "Oh! I'm sorry, Simon. I have to go! I'll call you soon."

After bringing the conversation to an abrupt end, she walked through to the breakfast room to scan the garden. There was no sign of Nicholas, so she wandered into the kitchen in hopes of catching him, red-handed, being pampered by Mrs Bottomley, but the housekeeper was alone at the Aga.

"Did you see where Nicholas went?"

"Who?"

"Nicholas, he came in a few moments ago," Julie explained, smiling to herself a little guiltily. Mrs Bottomley still did not know Nicholas's real identity. She thought he was the foreman overseeing the garden work.

"Oh *that* young man." Mrs Bottomley sniffed, plainly aggrieved. "He came asking for you. I told him you were busy on the telephone talking to your husband, but he just pushed past me. Barged straight past me, he did. Very rude, I thought."

Julie registered this information with acute anguish. She could almost feel the color draining away from her face. Her legs seemed to grow hollow and she leaned against the doorpost for support.

"You told him *what*?"

"How you were busy on the telephone. Long distance, too, I told him, but would he listen to me? Oh no. He just walked straight past me, as if he didn't believe me. Like he owned the place!" Mrs Bottomley was too absorbed in her feelings of injustice to notice Julie's distress. "Then he came out again, without even so much as a thank you. And I thought him such a polite young man, being so nicely spoken. But it's no good people being nicely spoken if they don't have manners to match."

Somehow Julie found herself back in the breakfast room, staring out at the garden, but seeing nothing except the absence of Nicholas. *What have I done? What have I done?*

Eventually she roused herself, collected her keys and left the house. Some explanation was called for and on her drive to Robert's house she mentally rehearsed, and rejected, several. Sonya answered the door, greeting Julie cheerily in a sing-song voice and wishing her happy birthday.

"Is Nicholas here?" Julie followed Sonya into the kitchen where trays of party food adorned every surface.

"Nicko? Of course not. I thought he was spending the day at yours."

"He was, but then he...disappeared."

"Disappeared?" echoed Sonya, casting a critical eye over a tray of empty *vol-au-vents*. "Planning his little birthday surprise, no doubt. I wasn't expecting you so early—there's nothing much to do just now. In fact, I'm wondering if I haven't started on the food too early—I'm afraid some of these things might become soggy by tonight."

Julie gazed at the food unseeingly and then left quickly before Sonya could focus her attention elsewhere and start asking questions. She sat in her car for ten minutes to gather in her own scattered thoughts before switching on the ignition. It's not the end of the world, she reassured herself. Granted, I should have told him myself, she acknowledged, but surely we've both been a bit guilty in that respect? Perhaps this wasn't such a bad thing. Now that he knew, they could put it behind them and move on like mature adults.

I can discuss it with him now, she thought. I couldn't have done that three weeks ago. That realization filled her with courage.

She hadn't been ready to discuss it before, but she was now. It was all firmly in the past and, thanks to Nicholas, she was now ready to move forward and face the future.

She spent further time in reflection in her own room until her attention was captured by the sight of Nicholas talking to two of the boys near the apple tree and she hurried downstairs.

"Nicholas, there you are," she called softly, approaching the tree as the boys dispersed. His hand had been resting on a low branch of the tree and she noticed his grip tighten so that his knuckles looked white against the tanning skin of his hand. "Nicholas, I think we should talk."

He turned slowly and she saw his face, hardened with coldness as his eyes gleamed angrily into her own.

"You think *we* should talk?" he asked icily. "I think that's something *you* should have done some time ago, don't you?"

"Yes," she confessed quietly. "I'm so sorry, Nicholas."

"For what exactly are you sorry?" He sounded furious. "For being a married woman or for lying to me?"

"Both, I suppose. But, you know, I didn't exactly lie..."

"No, of course not! You just failed to tell the truth."

"Yes, I suppose...rather like you..."

"No, Julie! Nothing like me!" He cut in, his voice like a knife sculpting ice.

She bit her lower lip unhappily and turned her face to the trunk of the old tree. Nicholas in his fury was frightening and unrecognizable. "What can I say?" she cried. "That it's not true? Oh, I wish it wasn't true. I can explain if only you'll listen...but...but, Nicholas, aren't you over-reacting? It's all in the past. Is it really so very important now?"

His eyes flashed with rage and incredulity. "I don't believe you asked me that! Yes, it's important. Correction! *Was* important. So spare me your explanations. If it's true then they can't possibly interest me now. You lied...you cheated us all. I hope you enjoyed your little game at our expense? Now you'll have to excuse me. I have more important things to do than listen to your lies." He turned to walk away. The contempt in his voice made her shudder.

"Where are you going?" She ran after him and caught hold of his arm, filled with panic.

He stopped at the old, weatherworn garden door which led to the side of the house and shook off her grip so abruptly that the back of her hand smacked hard against the flaking green wood and rusty nails. Realizing what he had done, he half-turned, instinctively, to try to prevent the injury, but was too late.

"Please don't leave like this. At least give me a chance to explain..." she begged miserably, but he turned away to unlatch the gate, ignoring her entreaties. Her own irritation at his continued stubbornness began to mount and she petulantly pushed the gate closed in front of him. "Okay then, go off and sulk! If you refuse to talk to me, I won't bother you any further. Will you at least make some excuse to Robert and Sonya for me? I won't be going to their party now. But I hope you enjoy it!"

He caught the hand he had so recently flung away and gripped the wrist tightly. "Oh, what will you do, instead? 'Go off and sulk'? No, I won't make excuses for you, Julie. You may have played your warped little games with *my* feelings, but I won't stand by and watch you treat my friends as shabbily. You *will* go to their party. No doubt, being nicer people than me, they'll be more willing to listen to whatever pathetic explanation you can dream up to excuse your lies."

"Then *I'll* telephone Sonya now," she muttered through teeth clenched, partly because of anger at his chauvinistic arrogance and partly because of pain from his grip on her wrist. As much as she cared for him, she would not allow him to dictate to her.

"No, you won't. You'll face her *and* Bob and give your explanations in person. It's the very *least* you can do," he said scathingly. He examined the bleeding graze across her knuckles. "And you'll need to put some antiseptic on that."

"*I'm* the doctor, remember!" she snapped in frustration, unable to pull her wrist free from his grasp.

Nicholas turned to call to the nearest of the three gardeners. "Steve, I'm leaving now. When you're finished here, bring the van around to Bob's—he's expecting you all early for drinks and you can wash up and change there."

Steve nodded a cheerful assent as Nicholas led Julie away from the garden and towards the kitchen door. Thankfully, Mrs Bottomley was not around to witness the indignity of Julie's plight.

"I'll wait for you in here," Nicholas said as they reached the sitting room.

"There's no need for you to wait," she protested, but he merely eyed her coldly and repeated himself.

"I'll wait."

"Well...then help yourself to a drink or...something," she muttered before escaping to be alone with her misery. As she was examining her damaged hand, she passed Elizabeth, with a wad of notes, crowned by her faithful laptop in her hands, on the stairwell.

"Goodness, what *have* you done to your hand?" she demanded. "Come with me, let's get it dressed."

"I *am* a doctor, Liz!" Julie snapped, feeling overwhelmed with frustration. She ran to the bathroom as the tears began to fall and her sister gazed after her in puzzlement.

Julie cleaned her hand and cried away all her tears under the steady hot stream of the shower. She reproached herself over and over for not having cleared up all their misunderstandings about her. Nicholas was right—it *was* the same as lying. And like all liars, now that she had been found out, she felt humiliated and ashamed.

How on earth was she going to persuade Nicholas to calm down for long enough to make him understand how irrelevant the past was in view of how she felt about him? There was no longer any doubt in her mind now that she loved him and that he loved her in exactly the same, extraordinary, undeniable, beautiful way. The totality of that feeling left no room to dwell on the past. They belonged together in a way she could never have imagined possible before she had met him. She knew that with a conviction almost too deep for words.

Of course, she had never known love before, because she had not known Nicholas before. And so she had made her mistakes. Everyone made mistakes—it was impossible to go through life without making them. If Nicholas had made a similar misjudgment, she would hardly punish him with the coldness and cruelty he was inflicting on her. It was an overreaction. A sign of immaturity, too, because everyone knew people grew through their mistakes. She would just have to find a way to make him understand.

Back in her room, she lightly applied some make up and then surveyed the silky dress she had planned to wear that evening. It was a beautiful dress in rich, fiery colors—a seductive dress, so carefully chosen for Nicholas and a night of love and passion. She tossed it aside in anger and picked out a simpler cotton dress with tiny printed blue flowers, which looked demure and slightly old fashioned. Not the sexy, raunchy love-goddess she had planned at all. She also tied back her damp hair with a heavy, antique clasp. She looked young and vulnerable, but her appearance had no visible effect on Nicholas when she returned to the sitting room to find him engrossed in conversation with Elizabeth about the latest problem the new clinic was facing.

She waited patiently as Nicholas virtually ignored her, but for the merest tilt of his head when she first entered the room, so that she knew he had seen her, but was deliberately keeping her waiting.

Her irritation peaked again when Nicholas took her car keys, which she had been idly dangling from her fingers, swaying gently, pendulum-like as she waited for him to finish conversing with her sister, who was far too wrapped up in his charms to tune into Julie's body language. When he did graciously extricate himself, he led her to her car, helping her into the passenger seat. Like most men, he preferred to drive than be driven, but what an arrogant, chauvinistic gesture! She swallowed her annoyance, however, in order to deny him the satisfaction of more supercilious remarks and neither spoke on the short journey to Robert's house.

I'm really seeing a new side to Nicholas's character, she thought sadly. *I want the old one back.*

As soon as they arrived, Nicholas disappeared in the direction of his own room to shower and change, leaving Julie gazing sorrowfully after him, wondering if she dare follow and plead her case. She had spent so many nights with Nicholas in that far corner of the house that she had begun to feel a sense of ownership or belonging. Often she had played the wifely role of tidying up, sorting laundry, cleaning the adjoining bathroom and lovingly arranging small vases of flowers and scented candles.

She knew every part of it by now—how those shelves of airport pulp fiction concealed a panel of instruments that revealed an amazing treasure-trove of high-tech equipment, from an enormous television screen mounted flush into the wall to the state of the art surround sound system and latest video games consoles. When he first revealed these to her, she had rebuked him mercilessly for his decadence.

Most importantly of all, she thought of that king-sized bed in which they had, night after night, made love with so much passion coupled with such profound, such exquisite tenderness such as she could never even have imagined before and, without Nicholas, could certainly never hope to experience again. The prospect of losing him was beyond endurance.

Julie gazed at the mountain of food in Sonya's kitchen and began to feel sick.

"Has Nicko given you his gift yet?" Sonya quizzed mischievously as she handed Julie an apron to protect her dress.

Julie shook her head dumbly. She tried to remember when she had last felt so unhappy and then realized that what she should be trying to remember was when in her life she had ever felt happier than these last few weeks with Nicholas. That was an easy one— never. She was used to unhappiness. Ever since her mother's death, it had been her constant companion. What she was not accustomed to was happiness. It was not so much the unhappiness of losing Nicholas that she feared as the sudden withdrawal of the happiness she had experienced through him. It was like another death, only worse. This realization caused such a stab of pain that she suddenly felt paralyzed and could do nothing but gaze at the butter knife in her hand.

"I expect he's planning to surprise you later," Sonya went on happily. "And Bob and I have a little surprise for you too...well, more a favor really. We'd like you to be our bridesmaid...maid of honor, I think they call it. You realize Nick's to be best man, so we thought how appropriate if you could be best woman."

Aghast, Julie dropped the butter-knife onto the work top and finally released the sob of pain which had been rising like a tidal wave within her.

Sonya looked at her in concern, as if unsure whether she had offended her or not. "Oh, don't worry, I'm not going to insist on pink frills and lace or any of that sort of thing. You can wear whatever you want. But I thought as Bob's so insistent on this church wedding, that I might as well go the traditional route, you know. After all it will only happen once for me. Please don't look so *horrified*, Julie. We thought you'd be *pleased*."

Julie dropped her head and the tears fell in great wet splashes onto her hands as they rested on the granite counter. "Oh Sonya, it isn't that," she sobbed. "It's wonderful to be asked, but...I can't be a bridesmaid."

Before Sonya could move close enough to offer comfort, Robert appeared between the two women, stretching an arm around each. "My two angels," he greeted them cheerfully. "What can I do to help?"

"I think you should take Julie across to 'The Ship' for a drink." Sonya gave him a quick and meaningful nod of her head in Julie's direction.   "I'm sure Nicky will help me with these few sandwiches."

He glanced briefly from one to the other, nodded at Sonya, deftly untied the bow of Julie's apron and led her to the door.

A few minutes later, Robert was securing a table inside 'The Ship Inn' and giving his order for drinks to the barman. The small pub was almost empty so early in the evening and being in such close proximity to Robert's house, he was well-known to all the staff. The barman lingered to chat, but was sensitive enough to Robert's body language to move away after a brief exchange. In the meantime, Julie had managed to compose herself somewhat.

"Sonya just asked me to be her bridesmaid," she told Robert in a flat, quiet voice.

"Is that what made you cry?" His voice was light and cheerful.

"Yes. I mean, no. Oh I don't know, Robert. It's just that, traditionally, don't you have to be unmarried to be a bridesmaid? Well, I'm not. And that's the problem, you see. Nicholas found out and he says I've cheated you all. I should have told you, I know it was wrong..." Her voice trailed away as tears threatened again.

"You're *married*?" was all Robert could say in his surprise. Then after a moment, he added irrationally, "You *can't* be."

She sighed. "It's true. I married in my final year of med. school—almost four years ago."

Robert continued to stare at her, shaking his head in surprise. "Four years? And Nick didn't know?"

Despite the irrationality of the question, she shook her head and bit her lower lip. Somehow Robert's repetition of 'four years' made it sound so much worse.

"Why didn't you tell us?"

She looked straight into his eyes. "I really don't know, now. But I haven't committed a crime. I suppose I just wasn't ready to talk about it. It's over, of course."

"Was it so...painful?"

"No," she said with an honesty that surprised them both. "Not at all. We parted very amicably. The marriage was a mistake from the start, we both realized that. I left him in Saudi. Perhaps that's why it all seemed so separate and, well, insignificant. It's in the past and he's in a different country."

"Who is he?" he quizzed, more for want of something to say than out of real interest, she could tell.

She gave a dry little laugh. "His name is Simon Gardiner—a surgeon, just as you all predicted, and probably the best friend I ever had before...before now." That much was certainly true. He had been her aide and mentor throughout medical school and her first exhausting and miserable year of pre-registration practice. Without Simon she would certainly have abandoned her career in that first, punishing year.

"But not the best of husbands?" Robert asked.

She shrugged. It was wrong to assume Simon was at fault—her innate sense of justice could not allow that. "Perhaps I wasn't the best of wives. Statistically, marriages between doctors have a very low success rate."

She'd married Simon out of a bewildering combination of gratitude and confusion. He had taken her under his protective wing and with his infinite patience and careful guidance had eventually turned her into a doctor. She had been very grateful at the time, only later realizing how crushing to her fragile spirit Simon's ambitions for her were. To confront her failed marriage was to acknowledge more than a failed relationship.

They both fell silent for a moment, mulling over their thoughts. One or two people entered the pub, deep in argument, which continued as they stood at the bar behind them. Robert shook his head several times and pulled his chair closer to Julie's.

"And what made you choose today to tell Nick?"

"I didn't! That's the awful thing about it. He found out for himself...and now he hates me. His reaction is completely over the top. He won't even let me explain."

"It's a bit late for explanations though, isn't it?" Robert's surprised tone caused her to wince. "Damn it, Julie, what were you *thinking* of? You knew Nick's feelings about divorce. Not to tell him you were married and to string him along like this is just... dishonest! And you should know by now that you only get one shot at proving yourself to someone like Nick. Lose his trust in you and it's lost forever. Nick happens to be a very good friend of mine and you were the last person in the world I would have expected to behave in this...shabby way."

"But I wasn't *stringing him along*—that's horrible. It's just that everything happened so quickly!" Julie protested through her tears. "In the beginning, it didn't seem to be anyone's business but my own. You all jumped to your own conclusions and that saved me from talking about it. It's not exactly something to feel proud of. I just wanted to forget it. Of course, I liked Nicholas from the very start, but I thought it was just a...physical attraction that would run its course for both of us with no harm done."

"That doesn't sound much like the Julie I used to know." His scathing tone made her cringe in shame. "And your misjudgment of Nick does you no credit at all. You don't have *flings* with someone like Nick. He's never strung anyone along in his life. Did you never wonder what a guy like that was doing lodging with me? Then let me explain." He took a sip of his drink to afford him a moment to compose his thoughts.

"I cracked up badly after Linda died—I honestly felt my reason to go on living had disappeared with her. I actually met Nick through Linda—he was dating a friend of hers briefly, so we double-dated occasionally. We got on well enough but he is five or six years younger than me and we didn't have that much in common really, different backgrounds and all that, except that he loved plants. Really cared about living, growing things in a way I'd never seen in anyone, except my granddad, before. It's rare to find people like that nowadays. He started coming down to the garden center to potter around and learn about the different plants. The place was a lot smaller then. It's thanks to Nick's shrewd business sense that I've been able to expand so much these past few years, but that's a different story.

"I was surprised when he turned up at Linda's funeral and then at how much time he managed to spend just being around, always on hand for a word, a chat, a bit of company—a genuine Good Samaritan. At first, that's what I thought he must be...you know, some sort of religious nutter, but then I realized he was just an all-round good bloke. There were very few people I could tolerate seeing in those days...so few people have his sort of...sensitivity. It's hard to describe, really. He never intruded, just...made himself available whenever I couldn't stand my own company any longer and I started to rely on him to help me take my mind off... the torment."

The mental images conjured by Robert's words were almost too much to bear. Seeing the person she loved through the eyes of someone else made her yearning for Nicholas acutely painful.

Robert released a heavy, heartfelt sigh. "Five or six months after her death, I...decided...well, that I'd...just had enough of it all." He broke off and stared into his drink. Julie could tell from his fragmented speech how much he was struggling to speak. He had to clear his throat several times before continuing. "I drove out to Nettlesby Wood one night. I was completely calm and rational, or so I thought. There wasn't a soul around and I picked my spot very carefully and pushed a pipe into the exhaust and..."

Julie gasped in horror, her own misery for a moment submerged by the shock of this news.

He nodded grimly and continued. "It seemed like the easiest thing in the world to do. I never gave it a second thought. God alone knows how Nick found me there. They told me afterwards that another two or three minutes and he would have been too late. Anyway, not to prolong the story, when I came out of hospital, Nick had given up his penthouse in town and installed himself as my lodger.

"Very few people know about what happened, but I'm sure you'll respect that. I'm completely over it now, of course, so don't look so stricken, little Julie. The reason I'm telling you about it is because if it hadn't been for Nick, I wouldn't even be around now, looking forward to my second shot at real happiness with Sonya. Now tell me how that fits in with *your* picture of Nick?" he concluded.

Julie shook her head in abject dismay.

"There are very few women in the world I would vouch for to Nick. I obviously made a mistake. I felt *proud* to be able to introduce you to him. Not that he needs any help from me in that department, but the minute I met you again, I thought to myself *perfect! What a perfect match!* I knew he wouldn't be able to resist you. Well, not the Julie you used to be anyway. How could you have become so devious...so shallow? And when he met you, I imagine he thought he'd discovered you like some rare, shy little woodland flower like a wild orchid or a larkspur." Robert shook his head sorrowfully. "Instead you turned out to be a sly little monkshood."

"What do you mean? What's that?" She was almost fearful of the answer.

"Just another wild flower—beautiful but deadly poisonous."

She inhaled sharply and felt a pain in her throat.

"I'm sorry. That was uncalled for," he apologized quickly.

"No it wasn't. I expect you're right," she conceded dully. "And one thing I know you are right about is that I don't deserve him. If it's any consolation, I don't imagine Nicholas will suffer as long or as much as I shall. Look Robert, would you mind if we left now?" The pub had filled considerably and the noise was becoming unbearable for her head.

Walking back to Robert's house, she turned towards him again. "I don't know if I can ever make any of you believe it, but I really am desperately sorry about all this. Will you apologize to Sonya for me? I can't possibly attend your party or talk to anyone tonight. I feel I've been criminalized enough for one day."

They halted beside her car in the drive. He glanced up at the house briefly—it was lit up like a Christmas tree—and then at Julie. "What about Nick?"

"Nicholas! Oh, Robert, I've just remembered—he has my car keys!" she exclaimed.

He eyed her levelly for a few seconds. "I suppose you want *me* to go and get them for you?"

Julie leaned against the car, hugging her arms around her for protection from the chilly night air. The first party guests began to straggle towards the door. The garden center van was parked on the road outside the drive. A frosty-looking moon peered down mistily from the sky. It was almost full and she could discern the cold, opaque outline of its swollenness and the dark shadows on its nearly-round face. One or two stars splashed pin-points of light here and there across the heavens. No clouds filtered the flinty little spots. Somewhere in the distance, a bell tinkled flatly, or so Julie thought, until she turned to face Nicholas holding her key-ring between thumb and forefinger.

"You wanted your keys?" he asked coldly.

Her heart lurched sickeningly and she gazed into his handsome, hostile face. "Nicholas! Please don't let it end like this. I wish you would let me explain..."

"Explain? Julie, why can't you understand? I don't think there can be any possible explanation you could offer me right now which I could find acceptable for what you've done."

"You might if you tried hard enough," she said in a tiny, miserable voice but he merely held out the keys in silence.

She looked despairingly at the garden center van as she blinked hard to fight back yet more tears. "I can't get my car out of here. That van is blocking the exit."

"You did pass your driving test, I presume?" His voice oozed contempt. "Then you ought to be able to reverse a bus through that space."

"Sonya was right, you know, for a twenty-first-century guy, your ideas are really antediluvian!" she snapped at him before snatching her keys from his hand and climbing into her car. She slammed the door, switched on the ignition fiercely and rammed the car into reverse. Still biting back tears of anger and frustration, she struggled to maneuver the car through the allotted space as Nicholas stood watching critically, arms folded across his chest. Within seconds she had struck the van with the car's rear wing. She registered the sickening scrape of metal on metal before collapsing into tears over the steering wheel. *Dammit, dammit, dammit—couldn't I have just managed to do one thing right in his eyes?*

"Presumably, you failed the test," Nicholas observed, pulling open the door and indicating that she should get out. Wrapped in misery, she clambered from the driving seat.

"Nicky! Darling!" exclaimed a look-alike for Annabel Campbell-Turner—her younger sister, possibly. Her mannerisms were certainly very similar, Julie noticed as she watched the leggy blonde wrap herself around Nicholas. "I haven't seen you for *eons*, you heartless creature," the girl admonished. "Why haven't you returned my calls or texts?"

Julie shuddered as she silently observed the renewal of old acquaintanceship. This one, it transpired, was called Livvie, short, Julie presumed, for Olivia, rather than Olive. She wondered if all Nicholas's old girlfriends were blondes with fancy names and if she was the only plainly-named brunette in his seemingly extensive collection. With beautiful women throwing themselves at him like that, she thought, it's not surprising he doesn't feel the need to shift with the times.

Nicholas told Livvie that he had been very busy and suggested she wait inside where he would catch up with her shortly.

"Okay, Nicodemus, but hurry. We have so much to catch up on," replied the blonde, casting a cursory eye over the wretched Julie before moving in for a further embrace to emphasize her meaning.

Nicodemus? Julie turned and walked away.

A little further down the road and at a right angle to Lilac Close, was a short cul-de-sac in which a stark, rather modern church huddled in its meager grounds and Julie flung herself onto a wooden bench facing the rather uninspiring building. Thrusting her hands deep into the pockets of her light linen jacket, she surveyed her outstretched legs moodily as she pondered over the scene she had just left behind and wondered exactly how much 'catching up' there was to be done between 'Nicodemus' and the blonde siren. What she wouldn't give to be able to take Livvie's place in that embrace right now! Then she wondered if she would ever see Robert and Sonya again and her feeling of jealousy and desolation threatened to swamp her. She'd been ousted from paradise. What had been the name of that poisonous flower Robert had called her? Something beautiful but highly toxic, he had said. She wondered if she had ever unwittingly come across one during her woodland rambles. She suspected not. It took someone like Nicholas to discover rare beauties. You'd think someone of his experience would know the difference between a flower and a weed.

She gazed at a street lamp in front of her, watching the moths jostling for position as they flapped round and round. She thought Nicholas was like that light, attracting all the moth-like creatures, the Annabels, the Clarissas, the Livvies and probably many more, all irresistibly drawn to his lovely flame. He could have married any one of them and made the same mistake as her. Had he always been entirely truthful with them all? Had he never come close to feeling that intensity of emotion he seemed to have shared with her, close enough at least to have wrong-footed somewhere *en route*? Could he really know himself so well and be so perfect? Robert certainly thought so. He made him sound like a saint. Saint Nicholas—no, sorry, got one of those already—and he was a do-gooder too!

Some ten or fifteen minutes must have passed and Julie wondered if Livvie and Nicholas had finished 'catching up' and whether Nicholas had been left with sufficient strength to have maneuvered her car from the drive without further damage to either it or the van. Damage her insurance company would now have to sort out for her.

"There you are!" he exclaimed from a point close behind her. "I've seen to your car for you."

"And Livvie too, I trust?"

He actually managed the merest flicker of a smile, if it wasn't just a tic in his cheek, that is. Livvie's 'catching up' must have been very therapeutic, Julie thought.

"She's an old friend," he explained dismissively, to no-one in particular.

But not very old, Julie thought. Then she caught her breath as Nicholas came to sit on the bench beside her. At last he was coming to his senses!

"Can I ask you one question, Julie? Was it because you thought I was a simple gardener that you felt you had free license to trample on my feelings?"

She groaned. "Oh Nicholas, you *know* that isn't true."

"Then it seems I know very little," he replied dryly. "I suggest you go home now before you freeze to death."

She jumped up from the bench, her feet, in their light, strappy sandals smarting with the cold as she planted them solidly in front of him and gazed down at him. "My marriage was over long before I met you. It was a mistake that should never have happened. I was ashamed of it. It was like my career in a way. Passing your exams doesn't automatically make you a good doctor in exactly the same way that signing a book in a registry office doesn't automatically mean that you'll have a good marriage, or even a proper one! Simon and I were never really husband and wife, we were just good friends."

"Simon?" He nodded and repeated the name in a voice heavy with sarcasm. "Simple Simon? Simply making mistakes?"

Julie knew he was referring to her observation that sometimes people simply made mistakes in their choice of marriage partners, so the insult was double-edged. "You have no right to insult him." she reproached quietly.

"No, of course not. He's your husband."

"No, Nicholas. Not anymore, but he *is* my friend."

"Really? That's what I thought *I* was. It seems you treat all your friends the same way. Badly! In my book, friends don't cheat and lie. You should have told me instead of deliberately letting me believe you were someone…something else"

"How could I, knowing your views? I grew too attached to you."

"All the more reason for telling the truth, don't you think?"

"But I couldn't bear to risk losing what we had."

"We could never have anything built on a foundation of lies. If I asked your husband, would he tell me you were never really his wife? Would *he* betray you the way *you* betrayed him? Do you hate all men, Julie? Or is it that you *simply* don't know the difference between right and wrong, or the truth and lying?"

She was as wounded by his tone as much as his words but still pressed on, her voice little more than a shaky whisper. "I don't hate you, Nicholas. I love you."

"I'll leave your keys on the bench." His voice sounded icy.

She backed away a pace and stared down at her feet in misery. Was there nothing she could say to move this man with whom she had shared so much love? Had she really damaged their relationship so irrevocably? How could he have changed so much, her tender lover? Had *she* done that to him?

She wanted a glimpse of the old Nicholas to reassure herself that he had existed and she hadn't dreamed him up. This cold, hard stranger bore no resemblance to him.

When she raised her head, Nicholas was no longer there. She had told him she loved him and he had simply walked away. How much more humiliation could she take?

Very slowly she moved towards the bench and reached for her keys before turning and mechanically retracing her steps along Lilac Close, her eyes never lifting from the puddles of light glowing wetly on the pavement beneath her feet.

He was waiting in the shadows beside her car. She was not surprised to see him because she didn't doubt the strength of his feelings. But people who feel so deeply, also hold on relentlessly to their principles. She had none of his pride or dignity however and she walked straight to him, placing herself directly in front of him again.

"I'm so sorry, Nicholas. You're the last person in the world I'd ever want to hurt. I'm not a shallow person, but I don't understand your reactions. Is there *nothing* I can say to make amends?" She searched his face. She placed her hand gently on his cheek for a moment, feeling the contours of his dear, lovely face, but he removed it, equally gently and shook his head.

"Please go, Julie. That's probably the kindest thing you can do for me now," he said wearily and she finally realized that he was right and further argument was pointless. She had read that in his face. *You only get one shot with Nicholas*, Robert had said. And she had had that... and blown it. She would never do for him now, because she was flawed and not what he had every right to expect from life. According to his friend, he was far too good to accept the second-rate. He had set his standards high—how dare she think *she* had any right to try to bring them down by offering him damaged goods? He was, gentleman to the end, simply making sure he discharged his duties correctly in ensuring she got safely and neatly out of his life. He was a very organized person, after all.

And so, aching in her heart and wretched in her soul, without any further argument, she climbed into her car and drove off down Lilac Close. She even denied herself a final glance of him in her rear-view mirror.

CHAPTER SIX

"Lizzie...I've decided to go away for a few days."

"What, *now*? *Tonight*?"

"Yes, now."

"Where will you go?"

Julie stared down at her travel bags. "London. I need to sort out a few things about the house. I promised Simon I'd take care of it."

"I see. But why tonight? Isn't it rather late to be driving down to London?"

Julie smiled faintly. "Not really. After all, it's open all night. Anyway I feel like driving."

"I see," Liz repeated. "How long will you be away?"

"I don't know. How long before the garden will be ready, do you think?"

"The garden?" Liz echoed in surprise. "I really don't know. Not for at least another fortnight, I should think. I thought you'd spoken to Nicholas today. I hope it will be finished before the Paris conference begins, especially if you're not going to be around."

"Oh yes, Paris," Julie murmured vaguely. "When is that?"

"The third. And then, of course, I have to go straight off to The States—such tight-timing this year. I do hope Brendon will manage in my absence."

"I'm sure he will," Julie replied without conviction as she could not recall who Brendon was.

"Well *he* thinks he will, but that wretched Henderson will be very little use to him, I suspect."

Julie did not want to hear about Dr Henderson and his dubious results yet again, so she quickly kissed her sister on the cheek and gathered up her travel bags, promising to telephone Liz and let her know her plans.

It was one-fifteen on Sunday morning before Julie left the M25 near Heathrow Airport and joined the M4 eastbound towards central London. Twenty minutes later, she pulled into the small gravel drive fronting the house which had once been her marital home. The house had not been entirely deserted in the past year as Giles, a close friend and colleague of Simon's, had been in residence until two or three months ago. But Giles had been a tidy tenant and to Julie everything looked exactly the same as she had left it.

She groped about in the silent darkness until she found the main electricity box. Slowly the forlorn house began to beep and buzz with electronic life as the refrigerator hummed, the central heating kicked in, the microwave light flashed and the clock on the electric cooker began its tinny ticking. Julie closed the door of the empty refrigerator and looked around her kitchen. With none of the ingredients for tea or coffee to hand, she poured herself a brandy and walked through to the sitting room whose silence startled her.

She fell into a chair feeling vaguely ill-at-ease in the silent room. It was the clocks, she realized with relief—Simon's antique clocks, all watching her in broody silence. She hurried to the old grandfather clock and began to adjust the weights. This was Simon's favorite and indeed her own, if she were to confess any enthusiasm at all for old clocks. Simon had neglected to mention the clocks in his telephone conversation and she began to worry about their future as she watched the old pendulum swing with ponderous regularity. "It will have to be storage for you, old man, I fear. Just until Simon returns." Next she removed the carriage clock from inside the antique walnut cabinet.

Ten minutes later, she returned to her chair feeling considerably easier and less lonely as the five clocks ticked and whirred busily from their various perches in the room. She wondered if Giles had bothered with the clocks during his stay at the house.

On Sunday morning, she rose early and walked briskly down towards the Common which was already alive with dog-walkers and children with footballs. The sun was gathering strength with the passing minutes and by the time she had made her purchases in the small supermarket and begun the walk homeward, she was able to remove her coat and enjoy the warmth of the sun on her arms.

She busied herself in the house until late afternoon, that time on a Sunday when restlessness reaches its zenith, and Julie could find nothing to satisfactorily occupy her mind or body. She stared moodily at the television set which she had switched on without the volume but could not then be bothered to explore the channels. A middle-aged man was making a silent tour through the ruins of an abbey, gesticulating wildly with his hands to direct the camera to its crumbling walls and disintegrating architectural features. The clocks compensated for the lack of words. She tried not to think of Nicholas and the past few weeks of happiness. Just three weeks— was that to be her frugal allocation of bliss in this life? She knew it was too good to last, but surely, *surely* she deserved a little bit more than that? Clearly not, as even that had been stolen or ought never to have existed as she had no claim on happiness. She was a poisonous flower, a monkshood, beautiful but deadly.

The telephone shrilled and roused her from her inertia. She picked it up before the answering machine kicked in, but it was only a wrong number. Another mistake. Foolish to have hoped for anything else. She clicked on the answering machine and heard Simon's voice saying,

"You're through to the residence of Simon and Jules Gardiner, though you may know my wife better as Dr Juliet Somerville..." She remembered the message well, as Simon had recorded it just prior to leaving for Saudi and it continued in an uncharacteristically light-hearted vein. She flipped the record button and began to record a new message but after two or three stumbling attempts to recite a suitable message, abandoned it and switched it back to the original before turning off the machine. She also switched the telephone to mute and added the words 'disconnect phone' to her list of tasks for the forthcoming week. At the head of the list was 'contact realtor'.

Simon seemed sure that he would not be returning to the Ealing house and his Welsh friend, Giles, had now bought his own place, so Julie should dispose of it as she thought best. She knew she would not live there alone, even if she decided to remain in London. The house was too large for her and anyway, she needed a complete change. A small apartment would be all she would require, where she and her unhappy heart could shrivel and grow old together – true downsizing!

She turned again to the crumpled journals and re-read the advertisement she had seen, before taking a pair of scissors and neatly cutting around the lines of the box. She took the square of paper into the study and opened her laptop to update her CV and standard letter of application. She had to keep occupied to force her mind from dwelling on those blissful Sundays spent with Nicholas, but it was a painful task and the evening yawned ahead of her, cavernous, empty and dreary.

On Monday morning, she embarked upon her list of tasks, arranging firstly for a realtor to view the house the following day. She pushed away the memory of Annabel Campbell-Turner, which threatened to trespass. She must not allow it houseroom. The sense of emptiness she felt at the loss of Nicholas gnawed at her inner core, causing an ache inside her that was genuinely physical and made her feel quite sick. How could he have so completely filled up her life in such a short space of time to make the loss so acute? She felt as if she had been bereaved, but was denied the right to grieve. She needed to push all thoughts of him and anything connected with him away from her. The only way to cope with this intense pain was to refuse to acknowledge it and fill her mind with anything else but Nicholas.

She returned to her list. The electricity and telephone would wait until the last moment, she decided, and began to make an inventory of the things she thought Simon might like to keep. Her attention wandered to the unposted letter and she seized the envelope and scrutinized it, as if seeing it for the first time. Perhaps she should discuss it with Simon or Lizzie? No, Professor Robinson would be the best person to advise her, and she knew exactly where he could be found on a Monday afternoon.

A damp, sickly feeling engulfed Julie as she parked in the hospital car park. I seem to be swapping one malady for another—I never knew it was humanly possible to feel so wretched, she thought to herself as she traveled up in the shuddery old elevator to Professor Robinson's office on the fifth floor, directly above the medical wards. The last elevator she had been in had been a modern glass and chrome bubble that had glided effortlessly up to Nicholas's top floor office suite....

She tapped on the door and entered. Bertram Robinson was sitting behind his large desk, ostentatiously dictating pearls of wisdom to his secretary, Annie.

"Julie, my dear!" he exclaimed, rising from his seat and Annie jumped up and hugged her warmly before hurriedly leaving the room.

"Oh dear, I really ought to have telephoned first," Julie apologized, more to the disappearing figure of Annie than to the Professor.

"Nonsense, my dear, I've been expecting you," he assured her, stepping around his desk and encircling Julie's shoulders with his large arm. She was taken aback by this display of avuncular affection—he had justly earned his nickname 'Bertie the Bully' many years before she had joined his unit.

"Expecting me?" she repeated, puzzled.

"Yes, of course. I wondered when you'd seek out your old friend. Words cannot express how sorry I was to hear about Simon, my dear."

She stared at him, perplexed. Her old friend? And how did he know about her break-up with Simon? Surely not through Simon, who was the epitome of discretion.

"Yes...well..." she murmured, feeling herself color deeply. "These things do happen, especially in the medical profession. Don't they call it an occupational hazard?" The last thing she wanted to do was exchange clichés about her failed marriage with her old boss.

"This is true," he agreed, shaking his head sadly. "But nevertheless, it's so very distressing when it does happen—especially to one's dear friends."

She felt he was grossly over-acting and decided it was time to change the subject before he became maudlin. Perhaps he had suffered a broken marriage in the past and she really did not want to go down the road of reminiscences and comparisons.

"Professor, I came to ask your advice." She tried to sound brisk.

"But of course. *Of course*! It's not my subject, you know, but I've been reading up a bit on it and I've arranged with Ralph to be kept fully informed. I popped in to see him this morning. I expect he told you?" The Professor beamed with self-satisfaction.

"*Who?* Professor, what are you *talking* about?" Julie asked, suddenly feeling very nervous.

He eyed her skeptically for a moment over his bifocals, as if deciding which of his many tones he should adopt. He chose his most sympathetic.

"Why, poor Simon, of course. Who else?"

"*Simon?* You've seen Simon...*today*?" she demanded with mounting agitation.

"Yes, of course. I felt it my duty, poor chap. Knew you'd be expecting me to lend my support. He seemed quite pleased to see me...tells me you're ready for a stab at Part I. How's the old bookwork going?"

"Professor Robinson!" she shouted in alarm. "I don't know what you're talking about. Simon is in Saudi Arabia. He called me from there on Saturday."

The professor stared at Julie in astonishment as he considered her words carefully and then his own. He stalked back around his desk and spread his large, well-manicured hands out on its polished mahogany surface. He scanned them for a moment as if they were a script. Finally he removed his spectacles, placed them carefully on his desk and eyed Julie directly through his small, myopic eyes.

"What are you doing here, Julie?" His voice was measured and careful.

"I came to talk to you about a job."

"Then you really don't know?"

Her expression was clearly answer enough.

"Simon admitted himself on Friday night. He's down in Isolation now."

She stared at him incredulously. "You're mistaken, Professor. He called me from Saudi on Saturday." She found herself struggling to breathe properly.

"From the Isolation Wing, maybe. Saudi, no. I'm afraid Simon's in the acute stages of viral hepatitis."

"Oh my God!"

"Ralph Mayhew..." he began, but Julie did not wait to hear the remainder of his sentence.

She hurled herself down two flights of stairs and fled across the narrow bridge leading to the new pathology block, where she took a short cut through the Biochemistry lab. Using the fire-escape staircase she reached ground level sooner than any lift might and sprinted through the hospital grounds, past the old mortuary and chapel, until she reached the low, grey building on the outskirts of the hospital land. She flung open the doors and only then halted, gasping for breath.

"Juliet! Oh, my dear, I'm so relieved to see you." It was her mother-in-law, Helen Gardiner, who uttered the words before throwing herself at Julie in a fierce embrace. Julie surveyed Simon's mother, still panting to regain her breath. Mrs Gardiner continued speaking in a rapid, confused flow. "I only found out myself today. I don't think he wanted me to know, but Ruth called me—Sister Porter, you remember? But he won't allow me into the room until I've spoken to Dr Knight. Oh my dear, I'm so pleased you've come! Simon said you were studying for your exams and didn't want me to disturb you. It's such a relief to see you."

Julie stared at her mother-in-law in confusion as her heart began to find a more regular rhythm. So Simon had not told his mother that they had separated. How like Simon, wanting to spare her! But the truth will out...or will it? If she hadn't decided to come and see Professor Robinson today, when would *she* have discovered the truth? *No such thing as coincidence. What must be, will be.*

"You *will* talk to him, won't you, my dear? I *must* be allowed in to see him."

"Mrs Gardiner, Simon's worried about your renal status. He wants you to check with the nephrologists as a safeguard," explained the pleasant voice of Giles Fairchild in its musical Welsh lilt. Giles was Simon's close friend, colleague and recent house-sitter, with whom Julie had never managed to achieve much of a rapport. He acknowledged Julie's presence with distinct coolness.

"Hello, Giles. What's *happening?* How *is* he?"

Giles eyed her almost distrustfully before shrugging his shoulders noncommittally and indicated Simon's room with a nod of his head. "See for yourself," he suggested unhelpfully. "I'm waiting for Ralph Mayhew now."

Julie unthinkingly strode towards the room indicated.

"You can't go in there!" snapped an officious nurse. "Oh! Dr Somerville." Her voice softened in contrition. "You'll find the protective clothing through here."

Arrayed in an oversized gown and clumsy overshoes, Julie entered Simon's small room.

He was lying on a narrow bed, looking tired and uncomfortably out of place, his blond hair sweeping his forehead untidily.

"Simon!" she cried, hurrying towards her husband's bed.

"Jules? How did you..."

No such thing as coincidence!

"Why didn't you *tell* me?" she wailed and then bit her lip, recalling that she had terminated their telephone conversation without allowing him very much time to tell her anything in much detail. "Oh, Simon, forgive me! I'm *so* sorry. Tell me what happened." She pulled out a stool from under his bed and seated herself as close as was possible to him.

"There's not much to tell," he confessed tiredly. "I must have been careless at some stage, as well as damned stupid for not recognizing the signs sooner. When I did, I brought myself back here at once. Old Arnold was fantastic—arranged everything for me. I wonder if you'd give him a call for me, Jules. Just to let him know?"

"Yes, of course. How are you feeling right now, Simon?"

"Tired. Nauseous. Bit of a sore throat, you know, but not too bad otherwise. Have you spoken to anyone?"

"No. Only Prof Robinson."

"Ah, Bertie. Had a visit from his lordship this morning. Jules..."

"Yes, Simon?" She leaned forward and impulsively took hold of his hand, which he jerked away immediately.

"Don't!" he ordered sharply. "And maybe you ought to scrub. Are you wearing scent?"

She drew back. "Yes...does it bother you?"

"It's a bit strong."

She moved back further. "I'm sorry. Your mother is..."

"Don't let her in unless Knight agrees!" Another order.

"I'll talk to him myself," she promised.

"It's good to see you again, Jules. But when you come again, will you leave off the perfume, old thing?" He tried to joke but Julie felt his rejection like yet another slap in the face. Could she do nothing right by those she cared for? *If I asked your husband, would he tell me you were never his wife?* Nicholas had taunted cruelly. Would she ever be able to do anything right again?

"Of course, I will. I'm sorry, Simon, but I didn't know...look, I'll go down to the residency and take a shower now if it's bothering you."

"No, don't go just yet. I think I'm getting used to it now. It's your favorite, isn't it?"

No it's *yours*, she thought. You chose it, you bought it, I just got used to wearing it. "What are they doing for you, Simon?"

He gave a mild snort which faintly resembled laughter. "Bleeding me dry for one thing. And watching me as if I were some rare, tropical fish in a bloody tank."

"Poor Simon."

"Poor Simon? The one thing we are all taught to watch out for from our first days in medical school and Simple Simon misses it!"

"Don't!" she pleaded, again remembering Nicholas's cruel taunts. "It's not your fault! And you'll recover."

"Do you think so, Jules?" he asked without any enthusiasm.

"Yes," she assured him emphatically. "We just have to be patient, that's all." And yet again Sonya's words flashed across her mind — *what must be, will be.*

She followed Dr Mayhew into his chaotic-looking office off the Liver Unit. Neither had spoken beyond light pleasantries on the walk over there. Giles Fairchild followed behind them.

"Have a seat, Mrs...Dr Somerville," offered the sour-faced consultant.

Julie pushed aside a pile of journals and sat on a hard, black vinyl chair. She inhaled deeply. "Can you please tell me what you think, Dr Mayhew?"

"What I think?" he mused, raising an eyebrow and fixing a cold pale-blue eye upon her. "I think he has hepatitis, almost certainly viral and in the acute stage. You understand, of course, that we have very few results through yet, and until I've seen some test results, I'm not prepared to speculate further."

"Are you planning a biopsy?" she asked, nervously, simultaneously thinking, *I heard you were a cold-hearted bastard.*

His eyebrow lifted even further. "For the moment, I'm planning to wait for the liver function tests and IgM levels, Dr Somerville. That should give us a good idea of the exact extent of the liver damage and then we'll proceed from there."

"I'm...he...I mean, there doesn't appear to be any jaundice," she pointed out uncertainly.

"No," he agreed, turning towards the window so that his face was hidden from Julie's scrutiny. "And I understand he's AA negative. But his liver is definitely enlarged and very tender and his history is quite characteristic, I assure you. I might be able to tell you more tomorrow, Dr Somerville."

Julie rose, sensing the pending dismissal and anyway feeling too distressed to articulate further coherent questions. Now she wished she *had* studied alphabetically; that way she would have covered the hepatic function before nephrology.

She sought out the housekeeper of the residency and arranged to rent one of the spare rooms. She showered, using the hard, unscented hospital soap and returned by way of the dialysis unit, only to learn that Dr Knight had not appeared in the hospital all that day.

"The dinner looked awful," fretted Mrs Gardiner. "And he hardly touched anything. I saw his tray. I really ought to call Alice, she'll be so worried."

"Why don't you stay in Ealing for the night and you can see Dr Knight early in the morning? I've arranged to take a room here to be near Simon, but I'll drive you to the house now. Then we can see Dr Knight together tomorrow, if you like."

"Oh, yes. Thank you, my dear. Then I can return to Brighton afterwards now that I know you are here. I can trust you to keep me informed."

But Dr Knight made no appearance on the following day and the general consensus of opinion was that Helen ought not to risk the possibility of infection in such an environment. Her friend and companion, Alice, arrived and bore her off to Brighton after Julie's repeated assurances that she would keep her mother-in-law fully informed of Simon's progress.

It was late the following afternoon before Ralph Mayhew sought out Julie and gravely handed her the computer print-out of Simon's initial liver function tests, which she stared at in dismay.

"The damage might be more extensive than I had thought," he told her quietly. "Do you know if he's managing to eat?"

She shook her head.

"Hardly at all. He vomited this morning and began retching just at the sight of the lunch tray. He says even talking about food makes him nauseous."

"Anorexia is not uncommon, of course, but if it doesn't improve, I'll start him on intravenous glucose. You haven't noticed any neurological abnormalities, I suppose?"

"No." Julie shook her head fearfully, searching her brain in a frenzy of alarm. "What are you thinking...?"

"Everything and nothing," he assured her. "We'll just keep a close eye on him and continue the screening. Oh, this is my S.R. by the way, Andy Farrow. I daresay you've met before?"

Julie nodded towards the Senior Registrar.

"Well, if you have any problems, he's your man whenever I'm not around," Dr Mayhew assured her gruffly before preparing to enter Simon's cubicle.

Julie sank into a chair, still holding the sheet of results. A nurse handed her a cup of tea which she stared into in gloomy meditation for a long time.

The following morning, an intravenous glucose drip was inserted and Simon appeared more cheerful for a time. As the day progressed, however, he grew fretful and moody, alternately chiding Julie for spending too much time with him thus neglecting her studies, and then giving way to gloom and self-pity so that Julie had to muster all her fortitude to soothe and reassure him. He would curse the laboratory technicians and junior medics for what he called 'abusage' of his veins and the nurses for their constant fussing, but was ever watchful that nothing was omitted or changed from the routine. It's true that doctors make the most difficult patients, she reflected.

Julie fell wearily into her hard, narrow bed that night, to be awakened at two a.m. by a sharp rap on the door and her name being called. Giles Fairchild's Welsh lilt sounded more pronounced than ever. "He's just had a G.I. bleed. I thought you ought to know. Andy Farrow's down there now."

Julie dressed rapidly and hurried to Isolation.

"Is he all right?" she gasped breathlessly.

"Ralph is on his way," came the reply.

"But the bleed..."

He grasped her shoulders firmly. "Let's wait for Ralph. You may not think it, Julie, but he's monitoring every step very closely. I've never seen him more concerned about a patient. Simon's in excellent hands. He's extremely popular in this place, you know. Everybody is very concerned."

"I know! I know! Everyone keeps telling me!" she cried, trembling with confusion, fear and exhaustion.

Her trembling did not abate at the sight of Dr Mayhew, his clothes in complete disarray. He looked as if he had gone to bed fully clothed and suffered a whole series of nightmares. She dumbly stood aside as he held a hurried conference with his Senior Registrar before walking into the nurses' room to don protective clothing and then entering Simon's room. She waited, her mind feeling woolly and distant due to tiredness. She tried to pull her wandering thoughts into some coherent shape but they danced and roamed around just out of her grasp. There was a coffee jingle and snatches of Shakespeare and Nicholas's accusations all spinning around in her head, monstrously, soundlessly, yet filling every private space with its senseless, repetitive silent screaming tirade.

"Dr Somerville," Dr Mayhew addressed her as he pulled off his protective garments. She followed him into the nurses' room. "Yesterday you asked me what I thought and I told you I was reluctant to speculate."

She gazed at him blankly without replying.

"Well, perhaps I ought to tell you what I think now," he continued, his voice made unrecognizable by the weariness softening its tone. He released a great, tired sigh before continuing. "I trust you have heard of fulminant hepatitis?"

Her mind's eye roved across pages of text books, trying to recall what she might have read, but she saw only a jumble of illegible words and she shook her head slowly, aware that a tear was trickling wetly down her cheek. She had failed again.

"Yes. No. I'm not sure. What is it?" she whispered.

"A severe variant of infectious hepatitis."

"Oh." She let her head fall back against the headrest of the chair. "What does it mean in real terms? What can you do about it?" There were a lot more tears now, but she let them fall freely. There seemed no point in trying to mop them up. She suspected the supply was endless.

"Little more than we are doing right now," he told her, his voice thick with compassion. "It's pretty much a wait and watch scenario. Andy has already started a dextrose and water infusion and I've added in Vitamin K. If he has a further bleed, we'll pass a tube to compress the varices. Meanwhile all we can do is...wait and observe." He pressed his outstretched palm onto her shoulder and the gesture explained the unspoken words. "You look all-in, Julie. May I suggest that you go and get some sleep?"

"No. I must see Simon."

"That will benefit neither of you. He's exhausted after losing all that blood and the best thing for him is rest. He was very drowsy when I left him. And you'll need all your strength for tomorrow."

She rose wearily and followed him out into the mild night air. She could smell the sweet scent of some nocturnal flower in the hedgerow as she walked back through the dark, silent grounds with Andy Farrow. Before climbing back into her bed, she opened one of her text books at the index to search for fulminant hepatitis. It was a very short section and when she had read it, she wept again.

"Jules?" Simon said after a long silence. "Do you remember old Lebe?"

"Yes, of course I do. I often wonder why he never contacted us." She remembered telling Nicholas about Lebe in one of her diatribes about inter-hospital politics and the prejudices inherent in the system.

"He's dead."

"No!"

"Suicide, apparently."

"Simon, how do you know that?"

"One of the staff nurses told me. She kept in touch with his wife."

"Oh poor, poor Lebe!" Julie exclaimed sorrowfully.

"Yes," her husband agreed bitterly. "Poor bloody Lebe. He never stood a chance, did he?"

"He had such rotten luck," Julie agreed with a sigh. That was not quite the way she had explained it to Nicholas.

"Luck? He drew the short straw on everything. You call that luck? Everything this lousy, corrupt system doled out to him, he took and all we ever did was pat him on the back and say 'better luck next time'. We should have done something at the time, Jules. We had a responsibility."

"You did, Simon," she reminded him gently. "You more than anyone, helped Lebe. Remember that. You can never reproach yourself. He was very grateful to you."

"For what? A few lousy books and bit of coaching for the Fellowship?"

"And more, Simon. You found him a job! You helped him over and over. He worshipped you for that and he would be heartbroken to hear you speak like this now."

Simon lay in silence in the dimly-lit room for a while before betraying his emotions with a quiet sob.

"But it wasn't enough, Jules. He blew his brains out! So it wasn't enough!"

She hurried towards the bed and seized his hand in her own. This time he didn't resist. Tears were coursing down his cheeks, startling Julie, who had never seen him cry before.

"Simon, don't!" she beseeched in an anguished voice, but the tears continued. She dabbed gently at his face with a tissue. "Is this really for Lebe?" she asked, gazing tenderly into his eyes.

Simon sniffed. "Sorry, old thing. It's just this place. Might as well have stayed out in Riyadh for all the difference it would make."

"Stop it! How can you say that to me? You know you don't mean it," she reproached, all the hurt sounding in her voice.

He twisted his head from side to side, as if trying to burrow into the pillows.

"No, I suppose not. It's good to have so many friends around here. Except my mother. Jules, I wish you'd keep her away from here. I don't care what Knight says. She depresses me with all her fussing and moaning. I can't really cope with her fears."

"I'll try to persuade her to go home tomorrow," she promised. "But it's only natural that she should want to see you. She loves you." She saw little point in reminding him that his mother had returned to Brighton several days ago.

"What time is it, Jules?"

"Around nine," she replied, taking up her book and removing to an easy chair as she knew he would shortly drift off to sleep. She kept her books with her purely for Simon's sake, being incapable of concentrating on anything else but his progress, or lack of it. She watched him now drift into a fitful sleep. His discomfort was obvious as he jerked and twisted in his bed, occasionally kicking out at his sheet and blanket.

"Jules!" he called suddenly. She was at his side in an instant.

"What is it, Simon?"

"The clocks! Did you see to the clocks?"

"Yes of course," she reassured him. "It was the first thing I did."

"I feel like that damned cuckoo."

"Cuckoo?"

"In the clock. Stuck in its little wooden box. I think I'll fix it tomorrow, Jules."

"I'll bring it in for you. Try to sleep now," she coaxed, watching him fall limply against his pillows.

"How is he?" Andy Farrow asked, approaching Simon's bed.

"A bit feverish. I just wish he could sleep and get the benefit of proper rest," she lamented sadly.

"He's not the only one who needs proper rest," Andy replied as he quickly and expertly inspected the drip leads. "I think you're spending far too much time down here. Have you even had any supper?"

"I'm not hungry."

"That's what you said when I asked you at lunch time. Come down to the mess and have a bite of supper with me."

"No. He keeps waking and I don't want to leave him alone."

"Giles Fairchild is outside. He'll sit with Simon. Come on Julie, if you carry on like this, Ralph will probably ban you from visiting altogether."

So she rose and meekly followed the Senior Registrar out of the cubicle. Giles Fairchild, already gowned, waited outside the door.

"Any change?" he asked as she pulled away her hat and mask. She shook her head miserably. Giles swallowed hard and turned to study a fading poster on the wall. "It can go on for a long time, this thing," he told her quietly. She nodded as the tears spilled down her cheeks. Giles turned on her furiously. "And you'll be no bloody use to him at all at the rate you're going!" he accused.

She could say nothing. She felt the wall behind her and let herself lean gently back against it as she watched him silently.

"Tomorrow is Saturday," he pointed out and she felt vaguely surprised by the information. A whole week passed in a twilight world. A whole week since she had last seen Nicholas. "I'm off for the weekend and so are one or two of Simon's friends who'd like to spend some time with him. Why don't you take yourself off—get right out of the hospital—I won't leave the ward for the rest of the day, I promise you. And if there's any change, I'll let you know personally."

And Julie thought: whatever I do is wrong. Now she was monopolizing Simon and preventing his friends from being with him. How selfish! She was just a selfish, shallow woman, not helping Simon at all. *Would he betray you the way you betrayed him?* Nicholas's words returned again and again to taunt her. So she nodded her acquiescence and even managed to mumble a faint, but nonetheless sincere, "Thank you."

CHAPTER SEVEN

A bulky envelope, addressed in Liz's scratchy hand, lay on the mat as Julie let herself in to her house. She left it on the table while she directed her attention to sorting out her laundry and feeding it into the washing machine. Later she read Elizabeth's brief note, a short enquiry and explanation of the enclosed letter—*left with Mrs B. by your friend.*

She opened the letter. It was from Sonya and dated the preceding Sunday.

My dear Julie,

Please don't worry about the party, I understand everything now. All went well last night but of course we missed you.

I've been told you've gone away for a few days but your housekeeper is unable to say where I might reach you. If you need a friend, you know where I am.

Nothing need change about the wedding. No one worries about that sort of thing these days. I hope you will accept.

Please contact us as soon as possible.

Sonya.

Julie sighed over the letter, but without hesitation, walked into the study and took up a sheet of writing paper and her pen.

Dear Sonya,

Thank you for your kind note, she wrote and then stared vacantly ahead of her, chewing at the tip of her pen. Maybe an email would be easier? People expected those to be curt. But then she realized she did not have Sonya's email address. With another sigh, she hurriedly scribbled, *Urgent business keeps me in London indefinitely.*

But surely it would be easy to find a contact address for Robert, if not Sonya through either of their businesses? No time! She frowned over the archaic and formal construction of the sentence but shook her head and made no attempt to alter it.

I am extremely grateful for your kindness but don't think I'll be able to accept the tribute. Tribute? she wondered. Oh well.

Please forgive my rudeness.

Yours,

Julie

Without re-reading the missive, she folded the paper and addressed the envelope. She placed a call to Dr Arnold Jefferson in Riyadh and then telephoned Elizabeth but received no answer from the house. Nor could Liz be traced by the hospital switchboard and her cell phone was apparently switched off, so Julie abandoned her efforts, remaining in the house only long enough to talk to Arnold Jefferson and pick up fresh clothes.

"How is he?" she whispered.

Giles Fairchild's eyebrows knitted together and he pointed towards the door. Julie saw the deep lines of concern etched into his face.

"He's sleeping now but he's been...rambling a bit. Ralph was here half an hour ago."

"What did he say?"

"Not much he can say, really. He's added saline with potassium and started steroids."

Julie digested that news first.

"And Simon...you said he was rambling?"

"Bad dreams, I think. He's lucid enough in between."

"Thank you for staying with him, Giles."

He eyed her distrustfully. "I didn't do it for you. I've known Simon a long time—longer than you, Julie."

"I know...I just meant..."

"*I* don't abandon my friends!" he snapped, before stalking into the nurses' room.

Meaning I do, thought Julie wretchedly. *When I'm not deliberately deceiving them, that is. I walked out on the best friend I had and then I denied his existence.* She turned and entered Simon's room.

He lay sleeping, his breathing irregular. She crossed to the bed to take his trembling hand into her own. The unpleasant smell of ammonia pricked at her nostrils as she sank onto the low seat, her gaze fixed upon her husband.   Simon muttered something unintelligible in his sleep and Julie stroked his hand soothingly.

"I hope you scrub thoroughly after each visit," Andy Farrow remarked on entering the room.

"Yes, of course," Julie murmured, not lifting her eyes from Simon's face. "He's deteriorating, isn't he, Andy?"

Andy sighed and leaned against the wall beside the upturned bottles of fluids.

"Well, there hasn't been any improvement yet," he admitted quietly. "He's gone into pre-coma rather quickly—a result of that damned bleed, I expect."

"Can't we do anything?" she moaned, not for the first time.

"Yes Julie...keep hoping," was his simple reply.   "And reassuring him," he added as an afterthought. "Most of all he needs that."

"Jules?"

"Yes, Simon?"

"I'm growing thoroughly sick of this place."

"I remember," Julie said lightly, "when I used to say the same thing myself in my pre-reg. days and you always quoted Gardiner's law at me."

"Gardiner's law?"

"That's what I used to called it, your speech beginning with the bit about the center of excellence, then working through the long list of all its merits and ending with the sermon about moaning housemen ignorant of their good fortune in being a part of this fine institution."

He grinned feebly at her changing facial expressions and poor imitation of his voice during her short homily. "You always did exaggerate, Jules. You make me sound like a pompous idiot."

"You were emulating your great mentor, Professor Herbert Harold Berkley-Fitzgerald," she teased. "For which everyone called you his blue-eyed boy."

"Old Fitzie," he smiled. "He was a good bloke, Jules. He was always very good to me."

"True," she conceded mischievously, "and absolutely foul to everyone else. But it was through him you earned your title *Simon the Sensational—Virtuoso of the Scalpel.*" She giggled and saw Simon smile properly for the first time that week.

"Cut it out, Dr Somerville!" He laughed weakly, his pun sending Julie into a fresh bout of laughter.

"A sharp wit, too," she teased. "Remember those awful puns your old houseman used to make?"

"Freddie!" he recalled, shuffling himself into a more comfortable position. "Old Fitzie threw him out of theatre for one of them."

"He threw me out of theatre, too," she reminded him ruefully. "You took a lot of stick for me in those days, Simon. I wouldn't have survived a week without you. Perhaps I ought to switch to surgery. I should have a very easy time of it when you get the Chair in surgery."

"High hopes, Jules," he replied, shaking his head slowly. "You always were a dreamer."

She wondered to which of two suggestions he was referring—switching to surgery? Unthinkable of course. Simon becoming Professor of Surgery? Providing he lived, of course. She tried to sound positive. "Not at all. It's on the cards and you know it." But her voice was too brisk as it had to combat the hard lump she felt rising in her throat and threatening to choke her. Who was she trying to kid? Simon gave her hand a gentle squeeze before drifting slowly into sleep.

An hour or two passed and he slept peacefully without mutterings or fretfulness. Only his hands continued to tremble. Giles Fairchild put his head around the door.

"He's sleeping," she whispered as he crept over to the bed to survey Simon's face. He pointed to the door and Julie obeyed quietly.

"He looks better," Giles remarked. "More relaxed. Look, Julie, I just wanted to apologize for being so snappy earlier. It was a bit uncalled for and under these circumstances..."

"That's all right, Giles. I can see how worried you are about Simon," she assured him with a shrug of her shoulders.

"He'd be the first one to yell at me if he knew how I'd behaved."

"Don't worry about it. I understand."

"I've just persuaded Hennie to make some tea—will you join me?"

She nodded and followed him through to the nurses' room. Ten minutes later Andy Farrow joined them.

"Why don't you go and grab some sleep, Julie? He looks as if he might sleep through tonight," he suggested, accepting the proffered cup of tea.

But Simon did not have a peaceful night's rest and when Julie saw him on Sunday morning, she was alarmed at the deterioration.

The fetid smell in the room and Simon's feverish, incoherent mutterings in sleep and semi-consciousness were more than she could bear at times and she had frequently to leave the room altogether to gulp in fresher air to sustain her.

During the late morning, Mrs Gardiner arrived and Julie felt too helpless in her misery to counter her mother-in-law's demands, so she strolled around the hospital grounds vaguely wondering at the sudden burst of summer evident in the flora and fauna around her, but incapable of enjoying any part of it.

On entering the lower corridor of the old medical block, she came across a public call box and made a reverse-charge phone call to Elizabeth, reliving her misery as she related the past week's events and begged her to come. Liz sounded too shocked and concerned to offer much consolation, but promised her sister she would leave as quickly as possible and join her in London.

Julie turned back towards the Isolation Wing, where all her shattered strength had to be summoned to cope with her near-hysterical mother-in-law. With the help of Andy Farrow and Giles Fairchild, Julie eventually managed to usher Mrs Gardiner into the waiting car where the faithful Alice took charge.

"Are you permanently on call?" she asked Andy Farrow in a feeble attempt at levity and because to have expressed her gratitude would certainly have reduced her to tears.

"For this case, yes," he answered, pushing open the door of the Isolation Wing.

The afternoon rolled slowly onward as Simon drifted in and out of consciousness and Julie kept her vigil.

"What's *he* doing here?" Simon shouted suddenly, causing Julie to start forward in alarm.

"What? Who, Simon?"

"Him! That damned beggar. I don't want him here."

Julie looked around her feeling helpless and trying to reign in her confused and weary thoughts.

"I'll send him away, Simon," she promised, grasping his hand firmly.

"Give him some money and the poor sod will go," Simon muttered before losing consciousness again. Julie began to sob as she listened to his heaving, labored breaths.

"Oh God," she whispered. "Dear God, please help him."

She felt a strong hand gripping her shoulder.

"There's a pot of coffee waiting outside," Giles said. "I'll sit with him now."

Julie sat at the desk, slowly sipping coffee salted by her tears, but she was unaware of both the coffee and the tears. Pushing the cup aside, she let her head fall onto her folded arms on the desk and began to pray to some mysterious, formless power who, for want of a better, she named God.

She started suddenly at the sound of movement in the room and realized she had drifted off to sleep. "What time is it?" she asked hoarsely.

"Nearly ten."

"Oh Giles, I'm sorry!" she gasped, blinking at the light from the inner doorway where a nursing assistant had appeared holding a tray of fresh coffee.

"I'm sure you needed it," he replied dismissively.

"How...?"

Giles shook his head.

"Not much change. But he keeps asking about some old beggar."

Julie nodded, pressing her fingers to her forehead.

"He was an old man in Riyadh. Simon gave him some money one day and the old man followed him around everywhere. He'd lost an arm and a leg, but he still managed to move around pretty quickly. Simon just kept giving him more money instead of sending him away. He felt sorry for him."

"I see," Giles murmured, pouring out the coffee and offering a cup to Julie. "Typical of old Simon."

"Yes." Julie smiled faintly. "Arnold—Dr Jefferson, who ran the clinic out there—was always nagging Simon about it. He said the old man was quite capable of doing some light work and Simon was merely encouraging his laziness—turning him into a professional beggar, he called it. I'd better go in to him."

"Don't worry. Andy is in there at the moment. He'll let us know when he's through."

"He's been so good..."

"Nothing more than Simon deserves. Julie, do you mind if I ask you something? What went wrong between you and Simon?"

Caught unawares, Julie gazed into her coffee cup to reflect for a moment.

"I think I just started to grow up. I think when I married Simon I must have been looking for a surrogate father. I know that sounds immature, but I *was* immature...and confused. He was my best friend too and he'd been so kind to me, but that wasn't a proper basis for a marriage."

"It looked sound enough at your wedding," Giles pointed out with some of the old acerbity returning to his voice. "I was his best man, remember?"

"Of course, I do. And Simon was *my* best friend as well, Giles. He always will be. I never said it was his fault and I'm perfectly willing to take all the blame if it makes you feel any happier! But I had a lot of time to think out in Saudi—time to think about what *I* wanted for the first time in my life. I suppose he told you how much I wanted to give up medicine?"

"Give up medicine after all these years? Are you crazy?" he demanded.

"Yes, I think I am a little. Aren't we all? Simon didn't think I was crazy though. Or maybe he did. How could I possibly know as he refused, point blank, to discuss it? That's what I meant about not having a proper basis for a marriage."

"Perhaps he thought you'd grow out of that too. He didn't oppose you when you refused to do more surgery and chose to join Professor Robinson's medical rotation. In fact, he couldn't have been more supportive." Giles clearly found it impossible to keep the edge of sarcasm from his voice.

Julie surveyed her coffee mug, clasped between her hands on the table. "This is more like old times, isn't it, Giles? You never accepted me as Simon's wife anyway."

"And wasn't I right?" he asked, grimly triumphant.

"I suppose so," she conceded. "But then I'm not entirely sure how qualified you are to judge. How come *you* never married, Giles?" As soon as she had uttered the words, she winced in shame and embarrassment as she saw comprehension dawn in Giles' face. "Oh God, I didn't mean to imply...I'm so sorry, Giles! Simon would hate this bickering between us—we have to think about *him* right now."

Andy Farrow entered the room and dropped heavily into a chair. "He's sinking into coma pretty rapidly," he told them dully, clearly unaware of what confrontation he had fortuitously interrupted. "I'd better call Ralph. He asked me to."

Julie fled from the room and rushed to Simon's bedside. "Simon, *wake up!*" she shouted frenziedly. "For God's sake, *wake up!*"

His eyelids flickered for an instant as he tried to open them. "What God?" he mumbled in a hoarse and barely coherent whisper. "Just old Lebe and a few stinking beggars." His eyes closed again and his head dropped sideways onto his pillow.

Julie spent all that night talking to him in feverish excitement as she stilled his shaking hand with her firm grip. What she said she would never fully recollect afterwards, but on she talked, hoping to strike a vital note of recognition in the deep, sleeping center of his mind and rouse him from his slumbers. When she could think of nothing familiar, she read sonnet after sonnet from her mother's little book, eagerly explaining, deconstructing, sharing all her thoughts with him. Once or twice his eyes fluttered open and he muttered a few syntactically haphazard sentences. When morning arrived, she reluctantly gave up her vigil to Giles without any further exchange of words, but left her books behind for Giles to seek comfort or find solace in some of Shakespeare's poignant verses.

After three hours' sleep, she resumed her vigil. When Simon called out deliriously for theater instruments to perform some ghostly operation, she entered his delirium, fulfilling all the other roles, from scrub nurse to anesthetist, repeating his orders and punctuating each with a firm squeeze of his hand, or responding to comments and demands in role, sensitively, never ceasing to hope that one of her responses might penetrate through to that vital, sleeping center of recognition.

But as the week progressed and his course continued with little variation, her own energy drained away and her efforts gradually subsided until she spent most of her vigils watching helplessly as he drifted ever deeper into seemingly impenetrable depths of unconsciousness. She lost all track of time. Sometimes she found herself wandering mechanically to the residency in the middle of the afternoon, when she had expected it to be late at night and being surprised at the bustle around her. Tiredness made her feel constantly cold and she would step outside into blazing sunshine which burned her skin and shocked her.

It seems I've missed the spring once again, she thought dully.

On Wednesday, Dr Mayhew sought her out and led her into the nurses' room.

"He's dying, isn't he?" she asked flatly.

"Julie, I want to try an exchange-transfusion. Would you have any objections?"

"Could it help?"

"It might. At least it's worth a try."

"Then do it! Don't ask me for my permission, just do anything, *everything* you can to help him. *Please.*"

The transfusion took place early on Thursday morning as Julie paced the grounds in agitation, finally finding a shady bench beneath a sycamore tree where she sat and immersed herself in her thoughts and prayers, oblivious to the bustling hospital, rushing about its urgent duty. She had read in the library that morning that the success rate of exchange transfusions was so low as to be almost negligible. It was clutching at straws. But then Simon could prove to be one of those exceptions to the rule—how typical of Simon that would be! And Ralph Mayhew would certainly not have advocated it unless he thought there was a chance. But then no one wanted to lose Simon, so everyone would, like her, clutch at straws!

She thought of a thousand things she wanted to discuss with Simon, some so trivial, she wondered how they had crept through the cracks in the door of her consciousness, like the remark she had made at the Christmas ball two years previously, but had refused to explain, leaving Simon baffled, and that silly, little quarrel with his mother's close friend and companion, Alice, during tea in the garden all those misty years ago. Then there was Giles and all the baggage around him that had caused such animosity amongst them. And had she ever really told him—made him understand—how deeply grateful she was to him for all his advice, friendship and caring?

To think that she, who had lost both her parents, should go on making the same mistake of taking this brief life for granted, never thinking that the time for explanations and apologies and ironing out all these little misunderstandings ought never to be entrusted to the uncertainty of the future. *Never put off until tomorrow what you can do today.* Wasn't that how the proverb went? It also meant never put off saying something important that should be said today! Why had she never properly understood that until now?

"Here you are, Julie," Andy Farrow said, sounding relieved as he flopped down onto the bench beside her. He was smiling. "Lovely day, isn't it? Simon asked for you, by the way."

"He did what?" She was on her feet instantly.

"Well, he called your name, at least."

Julie ran headlong towards the Isolation Wing, only stopping when she fell against the austere figure of Ralph Mayhew.

"Julie," he said, restraining her eager movements by a firm grip on her arms and waiting patiently for her to regain her breath before explaining calmly, "He's responding splendidly right now, but you must remember that the remission may only be transient."

She pulled herself free of his grip and hurried towards Simon's cubicle.

"Simon! Simon!" she breathed, grasping his hand in both of her own and hugging it to her.

His eyelids flickered lethargically. "Jules?" The word was no more than a whisper.

"How do you feel? Oh Simon, I have so much to tell you. Wake up, Rip Van Winkle. It's a beautiful summer's day and I want to talk to you." Impulsively, she leaned forward and kissed his cheek.

"Jules?"

"I'm here."

"The exam?"

"I'm going to take it, Simon. And I'm going to pass. For you." Silly, impulsive promise, but what choice did she have but to make it?

The faintest hint of a smile played about the corners of his mouth. "I know you will." The words were barely audible. "Arnold...?"

"He's coming. I called him and he's coming as soon as he can," she promised, tears spiking her eyelids. "Oh Simon, I owe you so much. Have I ever thanked you properly? It's time for me to start repaying now."

"You don't...owe...anything, Jules. Just...don't...give up."

"I won't. I promise."

She talked to him throughout the day and night, whispering to him in his dreams. Sometimes he roused and responded briefly, occasionally with questions of his own. For the remainder of the time he slept, often calling out in his sleep.

On Friday morning Giles appeared. "I've bullied the registrar into taking my out-patient clinic, so I've got nearly three hours free. You go and get some rest."

In adversity, they seemed to have struck up a new relationship. The animosity had gone, they were calmer, cooler, more mature in their dealings with each other as they apportioned out their time in the care of their mutual best friend.

Julie made her way to the residency, bathed lazily and slept until mid-afternoon. Back in Isolation, she found Elizabeth waiting for her.

"Oh Lizzie! Why didn't you get them to call me?" Julie threw herself into her sister's arms, overwhelmed with gratitude at her presence.

"They told me you were resting and that you needed it—and I can see that! Just look at you!" Liz clasped her fingers over her mouth as if to prevent her reproaches from escaping her lips as she gazed at her younger sister in dismayed silence for a moment. "But if you'd brought this, it would have been *so* much easier to contact you." She brandished the cell phone she had given Julie on her birthday, the latest in a large collection Julie's loved ones had given her in the past. Julie hated cell phones with a passion, a point on which Nicholas had berated her almost every day. This one was the latest all-singing, all-dancing device that practically lived a person's life for them and came complete with a year's pre-paid, unlimited anything-and-everything contract. Nevertheless, when she had left for London, she had forgotten to take her sister's present with her. She looked contrite, but Liz did not appear to be offended. "Oh my poor Julie, what can I say?" she asked instead, hugging her compassionately.

"Have you seen Simon?" Julie asked eagerly.

"Oh yes. And Ralph Mayhew," Elizabeth replied, leading Julie by the hand to a nearby seat.

"So he told you about the exchange transfusion yesterday and Simon's marvelous response to it?"

"Yes, but Julie, you must keep in mind that the success rate for exchange transfusions is not high," she chided gently. But then, seeing her sister's face, continued brightly, "But let's keep our hopes up. After all, Simon is a pretty remarkable person."

"He is!" Julie agreed emphatically, gratified by her sister's tribute, considering she had never approved of Simon. She fiddled with the slim phone in her hands for a moment. "How is everything at home?"

"Oh fine. The garden is finished, you know."

"How does it look?" Julie frowned at the memory.

"It's very nice—very natural and restful. I meant to take some photos for you, but I forgot. I was a bit worried about the fountain at first but it's absolutely perfect. It looks as if it's been there for centuries. But they haven't sent me the bill, though I've asked Nicholas for it about three times."

"Perhaps you should ask Robert," Julie suggested but Liz appeared not to hear.

"I wish I'd realized from the start that he was *the* Masserman, of Masserman Enterprises," she went on thoughtfully. "He's sorted out all the problems with the new clinic. Such a trivial business really, but how were we to know?"

"The clinic?"

"Yes. It was all some silly misunderstanding to do with sub-contractors but it had got so deeply buried beneath one administrative botch after another that the problems seemed insurmountable. All it needed was someone to trace the muddle back to the original problem. A trouble-shooter like Nicholas—he was onto it all in no time."

"Nicholas? Liz what are you talking about? What has Nicholas got to do with the clinic?"

"Masserman Enterprises owns the land. I'm sure I told you that."

"No, I didn't know that."

"And they always specify their own subcontractors, but some overly-keen young administrator thought he could undercut the contract costs. That's how all the problems started, though the source of the problem just became lost beneath a mountain of paperwork. However, it's all been resolved now, thanks to Nicholas. We have a lot to thank him for, Julie."

Julie nodded, thinking that if Nicholas had not reacted in the way he had that Saturday, she almost certainly would not have returned to London to find out about Simon. "I'm going in to see Simon, Liz." She hurried away, desperate to escape more painful memories.

Simon was sleeping rather fitfully and tossing about on his bed. Julie took his hand, stroked his forehead and talked to him soothingly. If this action did not comfort Simon, it at least helped Julie regain some tranquility of mind following the turmoil of thoughts about Nicholas. She returned to Liz after half an hour or so.

"Liz, would you like the keys to the house? I'm staying in the hospital these days."

"Is that really necessary, Julie?" Liz asked in concern.

"Perhaps not. But I want to be around, just in case he needs me."

Elizabeth sighed in reluctant agreement, as if knowing there would be little point in arguing with her younger sister. "Very well. My flight isn't until one-thirty, so I'll return in the morning for an hour or so."

No sooner had Liz left than Arnold Jefferson arrived, insisting upon seeing Simon immediately. Despite his exhausting journey, he remained late into the night with Simon. One of the VIP guest flats, opposite the hospital, had been prepared for him and there he retired for a few hours' sleep before resuming his vigil at Simon's bedside, making Julie unusually redundant.

"Jules?"

"Yes, Simon?"

"Did you pay him?"

She immediately thought of the old beggar man.

"Yes, my darling. I gave him some money. And Arnold has found him a little job so he won't bother us anymore."

Simon sighed in relief and drifted back into sleep. One less responsibility for him to worry about, Julie thought.

As the pale, iced shadows of dawn crept across the sky, Simon awoke again. "Jules, I've decided not to go back to Saudi."

"I thought you liked it there?"

"Yes...but enough is enough. We were better off here, weren't we?"

Julie bit her lip anxiously, guiltily. She hated herself for her lies, thinking Simon deserved the dignity of an honest answer, but she could not bring herself to hurt him. And anyway her sense of guilt was so extreme that part of her believed it.

"Perhaps. But if you want to go back to Saudi, I'll come back with you."

"But you hated it."

"As long as you're there, I can bear it. We'll do whatever you want."

He sighed and drifted back into sleep with the faintest hint of a smile on his lips.

"The light...it's blinding me!"

Julie looked around the dimly lit room. Only the meager night light illuminated its dreary interior. She threw a towel over it and stumbled blindly towards his bedside.

"It's the sunset," he explained. "So warm too. Isn't it breathtaking?"

"Yes," she whispered, close to his ear. "Remember how quickly it sets? Let's watch it together."

"If you like," he answered wearily.

She eased her arm around his shoulder and rested her cheek against his.

"It's fading now," she whispered, feeling deeply frightened. "Look, behind the mountain."

"I can't see it, Jules! I can't see it anymore."

Her tears spilled onto his cheeks, but she held him against her until she was sure he was sleeping normally, and her arm had turned cold and numb.

Giles Fairchild entered the room. "Oh God, Julie—you're taking far too many risks," he observed, lacking energy for a more spirited reprimand. "I couldn't sleep. How is he?"

She eased herself away from Simon, gently arranging his sleeping body and smoothing each limb with tender caresses before leaving the room. She stood outside for a full ten minutes in complete stillness and silence until Giles joined her.

"He's dying, Giles. He isn't going to survive and... Oh God, I'm so scared! I just can't bear to think how easily such a terrible thing could happen to someone so...so *good!*"

"You're just tired!" he rebuked. "What bloody use do you think you'll be to Simon like this?"

A nursing assistant came by with a tray of coffee and Giles pulled Julie roughly through the door of the nurses' room. He poured some coffee and added a large quantity of brandy from a flask.

"Drink this and then get yourself straight back to the residency and get some sleep. You look done-in."

But sleep was more exhausting than wakefulness as Julie struggled against one nightmare after another. Even before the sun had penetrated the morning haze, she was back in Isolation where Giles sat glassy-eyed over his morning coffee. He looked as if he had been crying.

"Any change?" She hardly dared to ask.

He shook his head and sighed profoundly. "Poor Simon. Poor bloody Simon," was all he could say and Julie shuddered as she recalled Simon had used the same epithet about Lebe.

The day passed in a blur of anxious faces for the weary Julie as people arrived and left again. After Elizabeth had left for the airport and the Isolation Wing was more than ordinarily crowded, Julie stole away towards her little haven under the sycamore tree where she was always sure of finding peace and solitude. She sat for a moment before unfolding the note Elizabeth had discovered waiting at the house and had brought to Julie that morning. It was undated and very brief.

Julie, all my efforts to reach you have failed.
Please contact me at once at the Dorchester
Hotel or on any of these numbers. Nicholas.

Beneath his name he had scribbled the telephone and room number and had added his office and cell phone numbers, the latter of which he had both highlighted and circled.

She looked up slowly through the still leaves of the tree and beyond to the spots of blue sky. Such a beautiful shade of blue, not unlike Nicholas's eyes. A wave of anger and guilt swept over her. Too late, Nicholas, she thought, I've seen inside your soul and I can't take on any more guilt right now. She crumpled the note into a tight little ball and tossed it into a nearby wire litter bin. She turned Sonya's letter over in her hand, feeling disinclined to open it and allow Sonya's homely chumminess to reach out to her in her present state of misery. Eventually, she clumsily tore open the envelope. This letter too was far shorter than she had expected and its tone was cold and formal.

Dear Julie,

Your letter has filled us with concern. Robert and I would like to help. Please call us if you need us. Nicholas is in London. I expect you will have seen him by the time you read this.

Call us soon.

Yours, Sonya.

"Sour grapes," Julie shouted into the leafy canopy overhead. She shredded the trite little note fiercely and watched the pieces flutter like confetti into the litter bin. Then she turned back to the dreary Isolation Wing, suppressing the urgent desire she felt welling up inside her to shout and scream and kick out at the world for its sheer, bloody unfairness.

CHAPTER EIGHT

Simon Gardiner died in hepatic coma shortly before four o'clock on Wednesday morning and Julie sat in his room for a further two hours, staring into his still, calm face. He had gone into renal failure the previous morning and Julie knew that all hope was forlorn after that.

She remained in the Isolation Wing for hours, too stunned to move or respond in any way to the numerous colleagues who came to offer their condolences and share their grief with her. She wished they would all go away and grieve in private as she didn't want the responsibility of witnessing any more unhappiness. They make me feel like a priest, she thought, as if I can give them some sort of comfort. She was appalled at her selfishness, knowing deep within her that all they wanted to do was express their sorrow at the loss of such a good colleague and friend, which was her loss also. But her grief and bitterness impaired her rational thoughts.

Giles Fairchild and Andy Farrow eventually managed to move her to the residency sitting room, where Andy poured out brandy and Julie's zombie-like mask finally fell from her face as she and Giles Fairchild wept in each other's arms.

Later, Giles drove Julie and her distraught mother-in-law to Brighton, where both women succumbed to the charge of the sensible Alice, whose masterly organizational abilities left Julie and Helen with nothing else to think of but their grief.

Helen Gardiner's mourning was all that an ailing widow losing her only son could be expected to feel. She grieved loudly and inconsolably, bringing illness upon herself to add to the worries of those around her.

Added to Julie's grief was a profound sense of guilt. Over and over she wondered whether or not she ought to say something to her mother-in-law about her recent separation from Simon. She recognized that there was little to be gained from doing so, except to assuage her own conscience. Nicholas's accusations haunted her continually and she wondered how it was that she had become so adept at deceiving people. She wondered what Nicholas might say about her double-deception.

It was Giles Fairchild, in the end, who persuaded her to say nothing. He pointed out that Simon clearly had not wanted his mother to know, so she owed it to Simon to continue the deception. Julie wondered whether Simon's motive had been to protect his mother or had he simply been too busy to break the news to her? On the other hand, he may not have fully accepted their break up as being permanent. There was also the possibility that Julie's leaving had been of so little consequence that informing his mother had merely not been at the forefront of his mind. Whatever the answer, which Julie would never know, mingled with her grief was a definite feeling of irritation with Simon for uncharacteristically leaving matters so untidily. Nevertheless she complied with Giles's advice and said nothing, feeling it was perhaps her just punishment to have to go through life with this added burden preying on her conscience as well.

The daily routine in Brighton was so simple as to wash blandly over Julie as one day merged gently into the next with little to mark the passing of time. The funeral was arranged at a local crematorium and Julie went along with all of Helen's wishes. It was a momentous day and Helen Gardiner derived great solace from the quantity and sincerity of the tributes to her son from so many colleagues and friends. She rallied majestically for the occasion, only to sink deeper into despondency afterwards. Julie spent her days alternately tending to her mother-in-law and wandering, in solitary contemplation, along the sea front.

Fifteen days passed after Simon's funeral and Julie began to feel restless in her cloistered existence, denied by the efficient Alice any other employment but that of ministering to her sick mother-in-law and, when Helen was again well on the road to recovery, Julie broached the subject of returning to London to sort out the house and what had now become known as Simon's 'estate'.

Having lost her only son, Helen was reluctant to relinquish her daughter-in-law, but even she realized her motives were purely selfish. After all, she and Julie had never been particularly close — how could that be possible with their vastly different lifestyles?

But Helen was deeply touched by Julie's parting gift of a little leather-bound volume of Shakespeare's sonnets, which she had found in a local antiques shop and which Julie claimed had given some solace to Simon when she had read them to him, night after night, in the weeks before his death. Here was a veritable feast to feed and sate the thoughts of a mother yearning to make contact with the thoughts of a son whose mind had been so removed from her own for almost his entire lifetime.

So Julie left Brighton and returned to Ealing, stopping first in central London to replenish her supply of textbooks for the forthcoming examination and also at The Royal College of Physicians to register her exam application in person, while her determination held strong.

At the house, amongst the usual junk mail, journals and medical literature lay a crisp, white envelope addressed in Sonya's hand. Inside was a wedding invitation and from within fluttered out a single, small square of paper bearing the message.

I hope this is forwarded to you wherever you are. Your house here has been closed up and we assume you have also left London. S.

Julie tingled with shame as she placed the card on her desk, without checking the date. She would write a long letter of apology to Sonya later. She then flung herself into a maelstrom of activity.

The realtor was called who surveyed the house and quoted a price far beyond her expectations, suggesting that the price could well be even higher if the house was sold with some of the furnishings, which suited Julie very well. She then called a furniture depository and supervised the careful packaging and removal of all the items that would not be sold with the house, including, of course, all Simon's clocks. She had not yet decided what to do with them. Giles Fairchild removed all Simon's surgical volumes for donation to the hospital library and helped Julie sort through Simon's papers and personal effects.

"What are *you* going to do, Jules? Why are you selling up?" he asked.

Julie felt a tingle of revulsion at Giles's adoption of Simon's pet name for her.

"Because I can't live here, Giles. My only plan at the moment is to pass the exam."

"Why?"

"Because I promised Simon."

"Perhaps you ought to be working—keep your mind occupied?"

"Don't you worry about my mind. Studying will occupy that very well."

"And after the exam, what then?" His voice sounded challenging, almost derisory.

She looked around the denuded study vaguely and shrugged. "I don't know. But I shall be thinking about it."

"Well, you know, you don't have to...I mean, if there's anything I can do..." His voice cracked and broke on a wave of emotion.

"Are you all right, Giles? I mean, you really don't look awfully well and..."

He broke into sobs and threw himself into Simon's chair.

"Oh Giles, what is it?" she asked wretchedly searching frantically around her. She seized a bottle of brandy and poured a clumsy splash of it into a glass. Giles swallowed it in a single gulp before he could speak.

"It's just...it's just...Oh God!"

"You need to talk about it, Giles," she urged gently.

"I can't get him out of my mind! I can't believe he's gone. Why him? It could have happened to any of us. Any damned one of us. But why did it have to happen to *him*?" His Welsh accent grew stronger in his distress until a loud sob strangled his voice. He reached for the bottle of brandy and poured himself another drink.

"I don't know why. But it did and you must accept it. How do you think Simon would feel if he saw you like this? And you know *that* won't help." She nodded towards the glass and then realized guiltily that she had offered him the drink in the first place.

He sighed and gazed up at the ceiling. "It helps a bit. It calms me down. You see, I feel so bloody nervous. Every time I go into theatre, I start shaking. I keep seeing his face in front of me and I think...I can't do this anymore. I don't even think I *want* to do it anymore. Not now that Simon's gone. Oh God! Poor bloody Simon!"

"Stop *saying* that, Giles!" she snapped angrily. She couldn't bear to link Simon's death with Lebe's because to do that was somehow to diminish the value of both men. Lebe who had suffered from what, in the name of fairness and honesty, could only described as nasty politics and blatant racism and Simon, the golden boy, for whom no door was ever closed, and who had only ever made one mistake, which had proved fatal. They were so unalike and yet now they were both dead. Prematurely. So it was natural that people would link them together. They had both sacrificed everything to a common cause. Death certainly was a leveler. She released a great, sad sigh. "Simon was unlucky, that's all. You need to talk to someone, Giles."

He gave a snort that sounded like a horse impatient to feel the wind in its tail. "The trick cyclists, you mean?"

"A counselor of some sort, maybe?"

He dismissed the suggestion with a derisive wave of his hand. "I always thought the best counselors were your friends. But just look what happens to them! This isn't about counseling, it's about survival. I don't care for the occupational hazards of this job any more. I just want out. Funny, but I thought you wanted the same. But then we have to confront the million dollar question—what else is there out there for people like us?"

Julie had often wondered the same. She had unquestioningly followed in her father and sister's footsteps, without ever really consulting her own feelings. It was expected that she would follow Elizabeth and her father—expected by everyone, unquestioned by herself. But then how could she question when she had never been taught how? Not until those grim and lonely nights when she had been called to certify that a patient was dead—an old lady to whom she had talked reassuringly only a few hours previously, a baby she had held and whispered soft endearments into its tiny ear, a child she had hugged and promised everything would soon be better— not until then had she learnt to question her particular role and, instead of listening to the answer from her heart, she had always listened to Simon, who had invariably always ended by presenting her with another question:

"What else do you want to *do*, Jules?" And she never had an answer.

Julie glanced about her and collected up the few remaining papers scattered over Simon's desk. She shuffled them into a neat pile which she placed in the center. "It would have broken Simon's heart to hear you speak like that," she rebuked mildly. "Why do you think I'm going to take the exam in November?"

Giles drained his glass and placed it beside the neat pile of papers. "Do you want the polite answer or the truthful one?"

"Truthful, of course."

"Because I think you're a coward and a hypocrite, Julie."

She stared at him too shocked to speak.

He grinned at her wryly. "I'm sorry, old thing, but I had to say it. And if it's any consolation, I think exactly the same thing about myself. I'd better be going."

She saw him to the door and watched him drive away. Even after his car had disappeared, she remained at the doorway for a long time, deep in thought.

Julie decided to return to the north following the visit from Mr and Mrs Laine, who came to look over her house. Their sensible questions, prodding and probing, were almost unbearable for Julie, whose mind rushed back to the day when she and Simon had first viewed the house and asked some of the very same questions and then forward to those visits she had made with Nicholas to other houses, in one of which she had secretly hoped beyond hope one day to share a life with him. How different their questions had been.

What a peculiar business this buying and selling of houses is, she thought...how many different roles we occupy as buyers and sellers and interested parties. And how much of ourselves do we invest in our homes? How much of our vital life-energy takes root in a certain spot? Do our souls return to the place in which most of our energies have been released, she wondered, gazing around her house for the last time. Would Simon's soul return here? Julie doubted it. The house was nothing more than a landmark, like the old milestones marking distances on the roadside and everyone accumulated many of those in their lifetime.

She and Simon had had nothing more than a business-like arrangement with the house. It had given them warmth and shelter and demanded nothing in return. Now these people, the Laines, seemed to expect a great deal more from the house than Julie and Simon had, because they were clearly looking for a home, not just an accommodation. Julie remembered Glebelands and realized that she had nothing to contribute to the house to detract from its cold, sharp edges and she thought the house would do far better if she left it alone to speak for itself.

On a sunny Thursday afternoon in August, she stowed her remaining personal effects into her car. She came across Sonya's wedding invitation, buried beneath the books on her desk and realized with a sense of guilty dismay, whose familiarity now bordered on resignation, that she had not written the long letter she had intended. To make matters worse, she saw that the date of the wedding was the forthcoming Saturday, making a written explanation now out of the question.

She pre-empted Elizabeth's return from America by two days, but Mrs Bottomley had already reinstalled herself in the house and was busy preparing everything for Elizabeth's return.

Julie spent the mild evening contemplating the transformed garden. It had far surpassed her expectations and on this golden, late summer evening, was a haven of peace and tranquility. It was a work of art indeed.

The following morning she ventured into the town in search of a suitable wedding present for Robert and Sonya and after several anxious hours of searching, eventually came across a small, triangular side table carved in rich, sleek rosewood and inlaid with an intricate, vaguely oriental marquetry design in lighter shades of satinwood. It was at least a hundred years old and beautiful and elegant in shape, and priced, Julie suspected, well above its actual value as it sat, unceremoniously, in the dusty small antiques shop tucked away in a narrow, cobbled alley. She had so far never seen any other customer in the shop. Even at three times the price, Julie thought she would have bought it for its sheer perfection, but the fact that it was so expensive assuaged her guilt slightly.

The table was a rather unusual choice for a wedding gift, but she could already visualize it in Sonya and Robert's house, as if it somehow belonged there and she was merely returning it to its rightful place. She knew nothing else would do. The proprietor offered delivery at no extra cost and Julie was tempted, but eventually she declined. She felt she ought to deliver it herself, with her own head on a plate on top of it, if necessary.

Early that evening, she drove to Robert's house in a state of acute trepidation.

"Oh Julie!" Sonya exclaimed, throwing open the door and surveying her friend before seizing her in an affectionate bear-hug.

The warmth of the welcome and complete lack of recrimination was almost more than Julie could bear. Sonya hugged and comforted her and dismissed all her attempted apologies and gently drew her into the house, assuring her that they were all alone. Eventually, finally, Julie relented.

"Bob's out celebrating—stag night, you know, though nothing riotous. And of course, he's not allowed to return tonight. We're doing it the old-fashioned way."

"But what about you? Why aren't you out celebrating with your friends?"

"Oh, I went out yesterday. I'm no fool, you know," she chuckled. "And far too old for the ravages of late-night revelries not to show on my face the morning after! I want to look my shining best tomorrow—and that's never easy, you know. Oh Julie, I'm so pleased you came back in time—I knew you would, of course. I just *knew* it, but it's still a relief. Now you must sit right here and tell me everything."

And so Julie did. When she began to explain, she planned to be circumspect, to edit out the unnecessary bits and just present the facts, but with Sonya, that was impossible, for Sonya needed to have every T crossed and each I dotted. She asked searching questions to satisfy her curiosity—not in a prurient way, but in a way that was necessary to help her to dig beneath the foundations of Julie's misery and carefully, lovingly, examine its deepest roots, the better to diagnose its sickness and offer the wholesome cure. Sonya's genuine but selfless curiosity was insatiable and Julie's need to talk overwhelming. It was only much later that Julie recognized what an expert counselor Sonya was and began to truly appreciate her role in Robert's life.

Two hours later, Julie started in alarm.

"Oh Sonya, what have I been doing, monopolizing you like this? Tomorrow is your wedding day and I've done nothing but pour out my misery! How could I have been so selfish?"

"Hey, listen, the most exciting thing I had planned for tonight was a chick-flick followed by a twenty-minute face pack and a simmer in the Jacuzzi. Now you tell me honestly, how much will a twenty-minute mud-pack enhance my beauty?"

"You don't need anything to enhance your beauty," Julie said warmly. "And Robert knows that better than anyone."

Sonya beamed. "Listen to you! I'd almost bet that he paid you to say that! A sort of compliment-a-gram, or something."

"Tut-tut, and I thought Robert had more sense than to choose a woman who had such low self-esteem!" Julie teased.

"Oh Julie, I'm so pleased you're home in time for the wedding, even if you have grown so thin you make me look like a fat frump."

At the mention of the wedding, Julie remembered the carton she had left at the door and jumped up to present it to Sonya. Delighted, Sonya ripped open the packaging and then gasped.

Julie interpreted her reaction as disappointment. "Don't worry. I'm sure you can exchange it for something else," she assured her friend quickly.

Sonya laughed. "Oh, don't *you* worry! I have no intention of exchanging it. I *love* it! Let's put it with the other presents, shall we?" And Sonya picked up the precious table and marched into the next room, indicating that Julie should follow. Julie did so, with misgivings. Sonya placed Julie's little table down beside its identical twin.

"Isn't it fabulous? Nicky said that he believed it had to be one of a pair and vowed to track down its twin for our first wedding anniversary. And *here* it is, a year early. Well, well! When did you find it, Julie? Before or after Nicky did? How did you know Nicky had bought us the other one? Did you plan this together as a little joke?" There was a distinct edge of sarcasm to the question.

Julie stood, speechless, gazing at the two identical tables.

"If you ever wanted to extend a hand of friendship to me, Julie, you'd do it right now by telling me the truth," Sonya said, gazing at Julie severely, her large face flushing with hurt and embarrassment and her voice almost choking on a sob.

Julie shook her head, still speechless.

"Only I can have a good laugh with the rest of them, but if someone is likely to come leaping out of the hedgerows to make a fool of me on my wedding day for some horribly embarrassing TV program or something, then I'd never forgive anyone who could be involved in such a trick."

"Did Nicholas *really* buy you this?" Julie marveled.

Sonya gave a frustrated little shrug. "You should know!"

"Know what? What should I know, Sonya?" Julie's eyes were glued to the matching tables, drinking in their every intricate detail. Of course it had to be one of a pair. They made such good sense together. The perfect pair! Nestled together they formed a perfect, neat rectangle. She let her fingers brush over them gently, reverently.

There was a long silence, finally broken by Sonya. "You really don't know, do you? But you must admit the coincidence is too bizarre. You can't blame me for wondering."

"Coincidence, you say? But *you* don't believe in coincidence! Oh Sonya! How could you imagine for one minute that I would...that Nicholas would stoop to..."

Sonya released a rather hysterical giggle and shook her head.

"Anyway, I see you also have other friends with similar tastes," Julie observed as she inspected the rows of identical woks, espresso machines and bread makers.

"No comparison though!" Sonya exclaimed through her laughter as she led the way out of the room. "At least these two are meant to be together. Oh Julie, I realize you're in mourning, but you will come to the wedding, won't you?"

Julie sighed unhappily and folded her arms across her chest, tightly hugging herself...holding herself together as if she were about to fall apart into a thousand pieces.

"Oh, Sonya, I just don't..."

"Please!"

"I just *can't*."

"*Please!*"

"Well, maybe just to the ceremony. I'd like to see that."

"But the reception..."

"No! Oh no, I *can't* do that. I can come to the church, if that's all right?"

Sonya sighed unhappily. "I expect so, but you see...well, I have a confession to make too. That letter you wrote..."

Julie felt a sinking sensation in her stomach as she recalled the cold little note she had sent refusing the honor they had offered her—*the tribute.*

"Well, it upset Bob terribly," Sonya said frankly. "He blamed himself at first because of something he had said to you and then he thought you might be taking revenge out on me because of it and that upset him even more. So...I... told him a little lie so he would stop beating himself up. I said you'd called me and that we'd sorted everything out between us. I felt sure there had to be some good reason for what had happened. Anyway, he thinks we've been in regular contact. As a matter of fact, he still thinks you're just avoiding...you know, Nicholas... and that you're still going to be my maid of honor."

"Oh Sonya!"

"Don't worry, I've sorted everything out. Petra's been on stand-by all along and she knows everything too. Bob will understand when I explain it all to him afterwards. But you must come to the wedding. I absolutely insist on that—for Bob's sake, if not mine. You owe me that much, Julie."

Julie paced the room for a moment to organize her thoughts.

"I'll come to the church," she said at last in a tone that would brook no further argument. "But you must excuse me from the reception. Please. I can't face Robert, or...Nicholas just yet."

A perfect day for a wedding, Julie thought as she wandered around the transformed garden the following morning inspecting every detail in its best light. Elizabeth was right, it was greatly improved and extremely restful, especially near the pretty old fountain which gurgled out the merest trickle of water and looked as if it had been there when the apple tree was a mere sapling.

The old apple tree, freshly groomed and clipped of many of its lower branches stood erect and proud now. Julie noticed sadly that the strong lower bough from which the old swing of her infancy had hung had been sawn away. The last time she had seen it, it had almost swept the ground in sagging despondency. How high it had appeared to her as an infant, but now she could touch the scar of its joint without even stretching up her arm. She rubbed the pale, circular wound and peered up through the leaves where a few muddy red apples dripped jewel-like through the greenery.

"You'll grow again, you dear old thing," she promised it. "And who knows, you may yet give some child rides in years to come."

All those 'rides' as she used to call them, on that clumsy, home-made swing that was better than any of the proper, painted metal contraptions in the gardens of her friends. "Higher mummy, make me ride higher," echoed the voice from her infancy. She let her cheek rest against the rough bark of the old tree.

"How much we've lost, you and I," she murmured, sadly.

She wore a pale pearly-grey silk dress with a delicate pink thread running through it and tied her hair back, perhaps a little too severely, with a fine black-velvet ribbon before shunning the feathery pink and silvery grey fascinator she had bought and donning instead a wide-brimmed hat with a tiny sprig of the palest pink flowers. She avoided looking at herself in the mirror. She knew she had become thin and was beginning to look gaunt. Like Elizabeth.

Creeping into the church at the last possible moment, she was halted by an usher in grey morning dress.

"Bride or groom?" he demanded. She hesitated, looking from left to right. The right side of the nave held more people than the left and anyway, she felt a curious need to support Sonya. And perhaps have a view of Nicholas?

"The bride," she replied, "but somewhere near the back, please. I have to slip away early."

The usher eyed her curiously as she selected her own pew on the left of the aisle as far as possible from the center.

When she had composed herself, she allowed herself to peer out under the protective brim of her hat and search the front pew, where, on the right, she saw Robert, looking slightly uncomfortable in his stiff-looking grey suit. His eyes scanned the aisle sporadically. And there beside him was Nicholas, elegant and attractive, bending his head towards Robert on occasion so that she caught glimpses of his perfect profile as he smiled reassuringly at his friend and doubtless offered reassuring words to match.

Time stood still for Julie. Her heart stopped beating and everything around her ceased to exist, as if in suspended animation. Still pause. The silent anguish of something ineffably sweet and cruel, squeezing the last vestiges of life from her wounded heart. Or so it felt in that moment before she remembered to breathe again and to drag her eyes away from the sight. Instead she stared intently at the printed sheet gripped tightly between her fingers until her breathing became regular, her eyes stopped stinging and threatening to spill tears. The organ became audible again and nothing but the remains of her sad smile played about her lips as the bride entered. There was a bustle of activity and the organist, without missing a single beat, switched tunes.

Sonya entered on the arm of a man Julie did not know. Behind Sonya, Julie recognized Petra who worked with Sonya in the shop. She was holding the hand of a small child of five or six who clutched a basket of flowers. Julie saw the smile of relief spread across Robert's face followed by a curious look, a frown even, as he glanced again but this was extinguished in an instant. She didn't see Nicholas's face when he too searched the aisle, for she didn't dare look up again.

Two teardrops slipped down Julie's cheeks as she listened to her two friends pledging themselves to each other for life and then as the small group moved off towards the vestry, Julie slipped, unobtrusively out of the church. She cried non-stop all the way home.

Photographs, wedding breakfast, champagne, messages, speeches, the cutting of the cake followed by more celebrations, perhaps dancing and then Robert and Sonya would leave for their extended honeymoon in Indonesia, first stop Bali. Julie followed it all in her mind as she stared at her textbooks and wiped away her tears. No wonder I've got so thin, she thought. I must have cried my entire body weight in tears recently.

There was a tap on her bedroom door and Mrs Bottomley's head appeared around the edge of it.

"It's that gentleman, Mr Masserman, asking for you downstairs," she said, extremely flustered.

He can't be! Julie thought in shock. Surely he should be at the wedding tying boots and tin cans to the wedding car or something?

"Please tell him I'm out, Mrs Bottomley," Julie replied, fighting to keep control of her voice and sound calm. She didn't even lift her eyes from her books, but that was only because she was concentrating on the painful pounding sensation in her heart.

"Oh but..."

"Say I've...gone out for a walk," Julie suggested. How could she possibly bring herself to face him and talk to him? She wasn't ready for that yet. The wound was still too raw.

Mrs Bottomley reappeared a few minutes later looking even more distressed.

"He...I'm afraid he wouldn't believe me. He said...just for two minutes. He promised not to take up your time. I said you were busy studying because I'd already told him you were in, you see..."

Julie rose and slowly followed Mrs Bottomley downstairs, patting her red and swollen eyes en route. His back was towards her as she quietly entered the drawing room and that gave her a moment to savor his nearness and take a deep breath. She felt like a wounded puppy being reunited with its owner. She wanted to hurl herself at him and melt his heart with her adoration but knew that was impossible. She'd missed her chance. Instead she tried to summon all her dignity.

"Hello, Nicholas," she said softly, closing the door behind her.

He turned quickly, took a step towards her and then seemed to change his mind and stopped. He seemed shocked and repulsed by her appearance and she was acutely aware of that.

"I've only just heard," he explained. "Sonya's just explained everything. I came to offer you my...condolences and ask if there was anything I could do to help."

"That's kind of you, but...no. Thank you," she said in surprise. *Offer you my condolences? Why? How horribly formal!*

He looked at her understandingly, as if that was the answer he'd been expecting. He was holding a small white card which he had been absently turning over and over in his hands as he surveyed her and he now placed this on a nearby table.

"Just in case," he told her, before turning to the door. "I promised I wouldn't take up your time and I'd better get back. Goodbye, Julie."

She remained in the room, feeling completely baffled. *Was that it?* She wondered what he had imagined he might do for her, and furthermore why, after what had passed between them, he should want to help at all. She remembered his role in Robert's life after he had lost Linda and wondered if that was the sort of help he meant. Again she remembered his words. *Offer you my condolences!* Perhaps he sees himself as an ace bereavement counselor, she thought miserably. He couldn't get away fast enough. As if he found me repulsive. Oh Nicholas, was that why you came? To gloat? Then you'd better have stayed away!

She crossed to the table and looked down at the printed card.

"So he chose The Cedars," she murmured out loud as she picked up the card. "I can do this. I *can* do this," she told herself firmly. "I'm glad for him. It was the best choice. Now I have a setting for him... I can imagine him in that beautiful house and garden." She sighed and compressed her lips tightly until the ache passed. "Better not, though," she told herself with a shake of her head. "It will only bring more tears."

On Sunday, Julie carried her chair and a small table to the apple tree and settled down to her books. It was a day for walking in the woods, not for studying, but she was fiercely determined to stick to the strict schedule she had set herself. However, far from inspiring her to the higher causes of medicine, the textbooks, along with the warm, persistent thrum of the late summer garden exerted a soporific effect over Julie's mind and her concentration wandered constantly.

Summer Sundays, she thought lazily, what a rich variety of activities a late summer Sunday affords. A day for families and friends to meet for idle pleasures, a day for sitting out on fresh cut lawns, alfresco lunches, ball games, fishing, swimming, walking, church and conversation. All those perfect summer Sundays of her childhood rolled into one. Even out in Saudi, Sundays were the best day of the week, the day when Simon usually managed to tear himself away from the clinic for a short excursion or few hours' relaxation with her.

Memories of the Sundays she had spent with Nicholas kept intruding, but she pushed them away. They were spring Sundays, not summer, yet now in her mind they had blended into summer, as perfect as anything she could conjure up. She wondered how Nicholas was spending his Sunday and relived that moment yesterday in the church when her heart had leapt in love and pain at that first, dear sight of him. But she must not think of him now. It would only bring more tears and she had had too many of those. She let her head fall gently onto her open text book and her eyes followed the skittering dance of a butterfly, which she allowed to hypnotize her into a light sleep.

She dreamed she was in church and making vows at her own wedding. But the groom was not Simon standing beside her. It was Nicholas who took her hand and led her out of the church where she found herself a child again, alone in a vast cemetery, searching for a grave, long-neglected, amongst broken marble angels and collapsing headstones. A faint voice called her name and she tried to follow it to find the grave.

"Mummy?" she murmured drowsily, suddenly opening her eyes.

"It's only me, dear," Mrs Bottomley was opening a step ladder beneath the tree. "I thought I'd see if these apples are fit for anything at all this year. Your sister is very fond of my glazed apple tarts."

"Where are the secateurs?" Julie asked vaguely.

"Secateurs? Why should you want those? There's nothing much to cut at the moment." Mrs Bottomley pointed out from the top of her ladder.

Julie looked around the garden in confusion. What had happened to all the asters and roses that used to rampage across the garden?

"Of course, *next* year," continued Mrs Bottomley, "they said we'll have flowers nearly all year round."

"Where can I find some flowers now?"

"The Garden Center, I suppose, though that shop in Lennox Avenue sometimes has a few bunches if you're not looking for anything too special."

Julie drove along Longshore Road, her mind still fixed on the sad old gravestones.

"Morning Miss Somerville," she was greeted chirpily by one of the boys who had worked on the garden. "Haven't seen you around for a long time. How did you like the garden?"

"Oh very much, Steve," she assured him with a smile. "You did a wonderful job. Thank you."

"Can I do anything to help you?" he asked, pleased with the compliment.

"I want some flowers."

He grinned. "Well you've come to the right place, then. Take your pick."

Julie selected and paid for her flowers and after a few further pleasantries, returned to her car.

"Oh dear!" she exclaimed as a sleek blue car pulled alongside her own and Nicholas stepped out. No such thing as coincidences, Sonya? How embarrassing! She shook herself for her lack of foresight. But how was she to know he would come here on a Sunday? She didn't want him to think she was trying to throw herself into his path and wondered if she should reassure him that she didn't need his bereavement counseling and wasn't going to resume her undignified begging for another chance. He had made his feelings abundantly clear. She nodded a brief greeting and climbed into her car.

"Hello Julie," he greeted, leaving his car and walking towards hers.

"Morning. I was just buying some flowers," she explained, realizing even as she uttered the words how fatuous they must sound, in view of the evidence in her arms. "For the cemetery," she added even more unnecessarily. She would have to work harder to conquer this awkwardness with him and stop sounding so clumsy.

He frowned in perplexity.

"My parents," she explained, pushing the car into reverse gear before turning it around.

She could see him in her rear view mirror watching her drive away, not moving until she had turned into Longshore Road and out of sight.

It was not as it had appeared in her dream, although the grave did look sadly neglected. As she pulled away the tenacious grass and weeds that had pushed their way through the green pebble chips, she decided to have the awful green stones removed and replaced with soil so that she might cultivate some flowers. Perhaps even create a tiny garden for her parents.

Two hours passed as she worked on the grave, clearing the weeds and the pebbles, arranging her flowers and trying to scrub away some of the dirt from the marble surround. "Next year," she murmured, "this will also be a garden full of flowers."

"Have you been gardening?" Elizabeth asked after greeting Julie with an affectionate hug.

Julie glanced at her dirty hands.

"Sort of. I've been down to the cemetery. The grave is a shambles, Lizzie. I've decided to do something about it."

"Another garden project?" Liz asked, raising her eyebrows and scrutinizing her sister carefully. "You look awful. You...you are feeling all right now, Julie?"

"Yes, of course. Must I be ill to visit our parents' grave? I should have gone long ago. There's something rather comforting about a grave. I wish now that Simon hadn't been cremated."

"What," asked Elizabeth suspiciously, "can possibly be comforting about a *grave*?"

"Oh Liz, if you don't know, then I can't explain. Don't you ever visit it?"

Elizabeth shuddered.

"Really Julie, this is very morbid and, if you don't mind my saying so, rather hysterical. I dislike the place. There's nothing there for me."

"Never say you don't believe in fairies for a little creature will die," Julie muttered half under her breath.

"What?"

"Don't you remember mother saying that when we were little?" Julie laughed at Elizabeth's expression of concern. "It's the same with the dead. We keep them alive in our imaginations. Ignore them and, *pop*, they're gone…vanished forever. *So long lives this, and this gives life to thee.*"

"Really Julie, you sound very…odd," Elizabeth rebuked, no doubt, thought Julie, making a mental note to pop into the Psychiatric Wing the next day. "And we've been holding lunch for you for over an hour…"

CHAPTER NINE

A week or so after Elizabeth's return, Giles Fairchild telephoned to ask if he might spend a few days with Julie and Elizabeth, arriving the following day. Julie agreed at once but was deeply perplexed about why he should choose to visit her above all his other friends. Certainly their relationship had improved slightly during Simon's illness, having progressed from intense antipathy to a wary tolerance, but he was the last person from whom she would have expected a social visit.

Giles looked altered to an alarming degree and little deduction was required from Julie to identify the problem. He drank excessively throughout his first evening and wept copiously whenever the conversation turned to Simon. His drinking did not make him unpleasant or belligerent, or even particularly inarticulate, but as the evening wore on his gloom deepened.

Elizabeth watched his every movement closely and with interest, carefully maneuvering the conversation away from possible problematic subjects and Julie silently marveled at her sister's sensitivity and skill, when she simply felt exasperated by her maudlin visitor.

After Giles had retired to bed early, Elizabeth turned to Julie. "He needs help, poor man, and he needs it quickly."

"He refuses to talk to a psychiatrist. I suggested that in London," Julie replied.

"Electively, perhaps." Liz looked thoughtful. "He has a typical surgeon's antipathy to them, yet he wouldn't hesitate to refer a patient in need to one. Typical of the knife-jugglers, and such hypocrisy! Well, we shall have to make him change his views."

"How?"

"By introducing him to the right person."

"Oh Liz, he'll just pack up and leave. Perhaps after a few days rest he might start to feel better on his own."

"He's clinically depressed, phobic and a seasoned drinker who probably hasn't got through a day without alcohol in the last ten years. What do you propose we do? Put Prozac in his coffee and lock up the booze? Be realistic. He needs professional help. And I know the very professional to help him. Alex Saunders."

"Never heard of him."

"All the better," Liz smiled mysteriously. "But from now on, he's an old family friend."

"Shouldn't I know our old family friends?" Julie asked dryly but her sister ignored the question.

"I've been intending to hold a little dinner party for a few close friends for some time. The timing couldn't be better. Just leave everything to me."

Julie had never triumphed in arguments with her sister and she knew when to give in gracefully, so she said goodnight and retired to her books.

"Why are you scowling, Giles?" Julie asked lightly as she joined him in the garden for coffee.

"Planning my revenge on old Will-off," he replied with a curt laugh.

"Mr Willoughby?" she asked. Mr Willoughby had succeeded Professor Berkley-Fitzgerald in the Department of Surgery but had not, as yet, acquired the professorial chair.

"Yes, old Will-he Won't-he, chief bumbler himself. Imagine being chucked out of theatre by that old fool!"

"It happens to the best of us," Julie reminded him with a short laugh.

He turned and smiled briefly, evidently acknowledging the memory of Julie's ignominious exit from the operating theatre two years ago.

She had been banned from assisting one surgeon after her third fainting attack, which had earned her the nickname *mop-head* in the operating theatres, as the theatre staff said her head spent so much time in contact with the floor. During her on-take evenings in her surgical rotation, Simon fixed the rosters and would simply step in and take full responsibility for emergency surgical procedures. This invariably caused resentment amongst his junior—usually Julie's senior—colleagues, but Simon was too well-liked and respected by junior and senior colleagues alike for any damaging repercussions to his unorthodox practices, and after all it was a win-win situation for everyone else, not just Julie. Without Simon's help, she would never have managed to pass her six months of pre-registration surgery.

"It happens to ten-thumbed fainting house-officers maybe, but not to Senior Registrars—at least, never before in my experience." Giles explained.

"Good heavens, Giles. What did you *do*?"

"Very little," he confessed wryly. "Which was why we came to blows."

"No!" Julie gasped.

"Well, *very* nearly, at any rate. So I was hauled before the wise men for insubordination and ordered to take some well-earned rest."

"You mean you've been suspended?" she asked in disbelief.

"Temporarily. To give me some time to reflect on the error of my ways."

"What went wrong, Giles?"

"Everything," he replied bitterly. "Every bloody thing imaginable. I'm like a nuclear bomb, just waiting for someone to push the button. I need a drink."

"At ten-fifteen in the morning? No, you don't. Mrs B. will call AA if she catches you at her sherry." Julie tried to sound light and dismissive. "I have a better idea. Finish your coffee and I'll take you for a long and very lovely walk."

They drove out to the woods at Nettlesby, which were resplendent in their early autumnal colors and walked along pretty woodland lanes, soaking up the peace and tranquility of the countryside. Two hours later they paused for a rest against the ancient walls of Nettlesby's Norman church.

"I'm glad you came in time for Liz's little party," she ventured tentatively.

He looked nonplussed.

"Oh, hasn't she mentioned it?" Julie asked with studied nonchalance, inwardly cursing Liz for delegating this task to her. "She's having a few friends around for dinner tonight."

"What sort of friends?" he asked, sounding suspicious.

She shrugged.

"Her team, I expect. I don't really know. Her friends, not mine. That's why it will be nice to have one familiar face at the table. You don't have to join us, of course, but I think Liz might be hurt if you refuse."

He laughed. "Put that way, I don't seem to be left with any alternatives. I imagine your sister's invitations are not ones to be refused lightly. And I don't fancy being confined to my room for disobedience."

"Does Liz appear to be such a tyrant to you?" Julie asked, smiling.

"Not really," he admitted. "But we all know the law, don't we? Consultants must be obeyed at all times."

"Except Mr Willoughby," teased Julie.

"Well he's not a magician, of course, but..." Giles fired an imaginary gun at his head and staggered back against the old stone wall.

Giles slept before dinner and Julie returned to her studies, waking him only at the last moment. She remained with her books as she waited for him to shower and dress so that she could accompany him downstairs and make sure he didn't bolt. But it was Julie who almost bolted as they entered the room together.

She stopped in horrified surprise at the sight of Nicholas, sitting apart from the larger group, deep in conversation with a pleasant-looking middle-aged man Julie had never seen before. She struggled to regain her composure, wondering what had possessed Liz to invite Nicholas, or what had possessed Nicholas to accept Liz's invitation. Hadn't he realized she would almost certainly be present in her own house, or had Liz somehow led him to believe otherwise? She wondered how she could make it clear that she was as surprised to see him as he doubtless must be to see her. Then she wondered if this was going to become a habit, the two of them being thrust unwillingly into each other's company, when she was trying so hard, so painfully hard to just forget him. Nicholas looked up before she had properly calmed herself and appeared to read some of these troubling thoughts on her face as he frowned and looked a little uncomfortable.

Elizabeth halted her conversation with her two other guests to make the introductions. They were firstly introduced to Brendon Foster, Elizabeth's Senior Registrar and his wife, Annette, an architect who appeared to be well-acquainted with Nicholas, as Julie later discovered. Alex Saunders was the man seated next to Nicholas and Julie almost died from sheer embarrassment when Elizabeth started to introduce her to Nicholas before suddenly recalling that they already knew each other.

"So sorry," Elizabeth laughed affably, proceeding to introduce Giles, who accepted a chair beside Alex Saunders.

Elizabeth drew Julie towards the drinks table.

"I did ask Nicholas to bring a guest if he wished," she whispered. "But he's arrived alone, so our numbers are odd."

"Why did you even *ask* him?" Julie whispered ungraciously, simultaneously thinking, *thank God he didn't arrive with an Annabel or Livvie in tow!* How intolerable would that have been, having to entertain his new girlfriend in my own home?

"Because he's been so very helpful, of course. Besides, I rather like him," Elizabeth replied candidly, pouring a drink for Giles.

Julie stared at her sister with mounting dismay. *I rather like him*! What did *that* mean? This was a fresh source of worry she couldn't begin to contemplate, so she turned back to the guests, feeling almost ill with foreboding about the evening's gathering and took the chair Elizabeth had previously occupied as Elizabeth settled herself next to Nicholas and began to chat animatedly.

At dinner, Julie found herself seated opposite Nicholas, with Giles to her right and Brendon to her left. Annette sat next to Nicholas and it was during dinner that Julie became aware of their friendship with each other. She was also aware that Nicholas was quietly observing her and her discomfort was intense as she, as co-hostess, in this uncomfortable position in the center of the table, was drawn into conversations to both her left and right. She exchanged very few words with Nicholas, though she could hardly avoid the regular, clumsy but brief eye contacts with him, especially whenever Annette directed comments across the table toward her. She could read nothing in his eyes, but she sensed they were devoid of the old warmth she had grown used to finding there. She would avert her gaze quickly whenever the embarrassing contact occurred and tried to occupy herself as much as possible with the conversations around her.

At one point, however, she found herself caught between three strands of conversation and could only respond with a burst of slightly hysterical laughter the moment her eyes met his. Once upon a time they would have delighted in the farcicality of the situation, she realized with intense pain, and that shared look would have spoken volumes to each other. But now there was nothing and it was Giles who turned towards her with a friendly smile.

"What's the joke, Jules?" he quizzed.

"None. I'm sorry, but this conversation is going like a crazy game of ping-pong," she giggled inanely, thinking that she could just as easily have burst into tears and that if Giles called her by that name again, she might well do so. "It's all so haphazard," she finished lamely. "It feels like one of those sessions where rules for speaking should be made. Only the person who holds the pepper pot up can speak at any one time," she finished, glancing around and realizing there wasn't even a pepper pot on the table. Elizabeth was frowning. Everyone else was looking at her with puzzled, polite expressions. Julie knew she was being ridiculous and ungracious. The animated conversations just proved everyone was getting along well. Suddenly Giles squeezed her shoulder in an affectionate gesture that took Julie completely by surprise and made her fall into a sober contemplation of her plate.

Fortunately, Alex Saunders was one of those open, extrovert men who automatically becomes the driving force behind a party. He seemed to know instinctively how to steer conversations away from their immediate collision courses with tricky obstacles.

Julie looked at him in gratitude on more than one occasion for the way he drew Giles away from certain subjects, such as embarrassing anecdotes of Julie's pre-registration days and eulogies of Simon. It occurred to her that Giles' sudden gesture might lead the gathered company to think that the two of them were an item and she wondered how to make their relationship, or rather, *lack* of relationship, clear to all concerned — or more specifically, to Nicholas. She would hate him to get the wrong idea, but nothing came to mind and she was obliged to dismiss the thought. After all, what was the point? Instead she focused her attention on Alex Saunders, whom she thought had real charisma and was genuinely pleased to see that Giles had taken to him as well.

She almost fell out of her chair with embarrassment when Elizabeth suggested leaving the men to their discussions while the women moved into the drawing room. Her horrified eyes met Nicholas's for an instant and she saw his amusement.

"You can't be *serious*, Liz?" she whispered, appalled, but then Alex and Giles seconded the proposal with cheerful good humor.

"Good," Elizabeth said smugly, ignoring her sister's stricken face. "You'll find brandy, whisky, port or whatever on the table just behind you, Alex."

"Oh Liz," Julie moaned. "What *can* you be thinking of? This isn't a Jane Austen novel!"

"Just a little baroque," giggled Annette in agreement. "But I certainly don't mind, providing we're allowed brandy as well."

"Of course," Elizabeth winked mischievously at the pair of them. "I've kept the best stuff for us. Oh do stop *worrying*, Julie. No one minded and Alex and Giles seemed to find it an excellent idea."

That was true, Julie conceded, so why had she felt so embarrassed? The answer tapped gently at the door of her brain, but she denied it entrance.

The drawing room door opened and Nicholas appeared carrying a tray of coffee for Mrs Bottomley, who danced about his heels alternately protesting and thanking him.

"It's the least I can do after such an excellent meal," he assured her smoothly.

"You're too kind, Mr Masserman," she beamed, fussing over the coffee table.

Yes, thought Julie, too kind. And too smooth by half. The perfect gentleman, whom I once took to be a simple gardener. Trust me to get it so very wrong! She wondered what had driven him away from the manly talk so soon, but could not think of a way to ask without sounding ungracious.

"How did you like the garden?" he inquired quietly, politely of Julie, taking her completely off guard.

She jumped up in anguish. "Oh Nicholas! How *rude* of me!" she exclaimed. "I'm *so* sorry. I meant to thank you. I think it's beautiful. I *love* it."

"Good." He seemed pleased. Genuinely. "I'm sorry we had to lop so much off your tree. I'm afraid it was necessary."

"It will grow again," she murmured, thinking that must sound like she was commiserating with someone over a too-radical haircut. She was still berating herself over her rudeness in having said nothing to Nicholas about the garden on the two previous occasions she had seen him when in fact she had so many questions she wanted to ask about it.

"How's your studying going?"

Small talk, she thought. We sound like strangers meeting for the first time. Have we really come to this? *Change the subject, quickly.*

"Not too badly. I try to aim for seven hours a day."

He raised his eyebrows. "Why bother with the exam if you intend giving up medicine?" He spoke quietly so that Elizabeth should not hear.

"It's...something I have to do. You wouldn't understand." She had not intended to sound rude or dismissive but the words were out before she could modify them and she wanted to bite off her tongue. *Damn!* Why can't I just behave normally with him, she agonized to herself. Everything she said came out sounding either ridiculous or rude.

Nicholas nodded and turned abruptly to Annette, directing the remainder of his conversation towards her and Elizabeth until the others made their noisy entrance, still laughing over some previous joke or witticism. Giles immediately crossed towards Julie's chair, leaned over her and kissed her lightly on the cheek.

"Witch!" he whispered.

Julie jumped to her feet in confusion for the second time that evening. Being kissed by Giles Fairchild might produce such an effect in some women, but Julie's reaction was less one of pleasure than of extreme consternation. Whilst she believed it impossible, she could not quite quell the nagging fear that Giles Fairchild might somehow have found himself attracted to her in some perverse misguided transference of his admiration for Simon—and the thought made her shudder! She glanced anxiously, guiltily at

Nicholas to see if he had seen the gesture, but she couldn't tell. He wore a mask of indifference. Giles put an arm around her shoulder and drew her apart from the group.

"Your little plot has been discovered," he whispered with a smile. "But don't ever let it be known in the smoke that I've agreed to see a provincial shrink." And with that he walked away from her and joined the little clan around the fire.

Julie sighed and in her profound relief, permitted herself a little smile of self-congratulation.

Nicholas rose abruptly, offered his thanks and apologies for leaving so early and allowed Elizabeth to see him to the door while she gazed miserably after him, feeling as if a light had suddenly been extinguished, plunging her into pitch darkness again.

Alex Saunders became a regular and welcome visitor to the house and, to Julie's astonishment and amusement, Giles Fairchild became a regular escort of Elizabeth Somerville. Julie occasionally joined the three of them in the evening, never failing to wonder at the improvement in Giles and the alteration in Elizabeth. She vaguely blamed Alex Saunders for capturing them all under his spell, but no reproach accompanied the blame.

With the passage of time, Julie hoped that her chance encounters with Nicholas would become easier to handle. If they were going to be thrown into each other's company, she would like, at least, to be able to face him without the attendant heart-tripping distress. Nicholas himself continued to remain aloof and composed, showing he no longer felt anything for her and this made her all the more determined to behave in a cool and dignified way. But determination alone seemed not to be enough.

The worst scenario she could think of finally happened one evening when Julie had reluctantly agreed to go with Giles to join Elizabeth and Alex for a drink at a well-known wine bar in the town center. She saw Nicholas even before she had taken a seat and her first instinct was to turn and run in a state of complete panic, but when she tried to follow her instinct, she merely came up against Alex, who propelled her into her seat.

He was with a woman, blonde of course and very attractive and her name, it soon transpired, was Antoinette. Nicholas made no attempt to qualify their relationship when he made the introductions, which omission seemed to suggest that it was an intimate one.

Julie felt crushed and could barely raise her eyes, so convinced was she that all the pain she felt would be clearly visible there for all to read. I *have* to get over this, she told herself miserably. Nicholas had moved on with his life and so must she.

But it was not an easy evening and when someone—Julie could not afterwards remember who, as the pain was so acute it rammed memory into second gear—suggested Nicholas and Antoinette join their group, Julie prayed only for the ground to swallow her up whole. She could see Antoinette was indifferent to the suggestion and so was astonished at Nicholas's insensitivity in accepting. Is he trying to rub my nose in it, she wondered. Did he think she hadn't seen them together and taken due note of how gorgeous she was? Or does he just not care? The sense of betrayal she felt was inexpressible. Angrily, she told herself that this was the best test possible—if she could just survive this evening, then she would have passed the worst hurdle of all. And unless she was prepared to take herself right away from home, this was something she *must* do! She couldn't become a complete recluse in order to avoid him forever.

But it was an evening of unadulterated misery for Julie and when Alex, or maybe Giles, later suggested that they should all go on to a restaurant together, it was more than she could bear. She waited in silence as they made their plans and then at the last moment asked to be excused, quietly but firmly, pleading a headache and lack of appetite. Everyone expressed their concern in different ways and then Elizabeth began to have second thoughts and remember her workload the next day, but Julie would listen to none of it.

"Just *please*, all of you, do what you planned to do. Go to the restaurant. I'll be perfectly fine. I'm going to call a taxi right now."

"I'll drive you home, if you like," Nicholas said quietly.

Julie stared at him in shock. She needed to exert all her will-power not to slap his face! Did he really think she was going to cram herself into his sexy sports car with him and his new girlfriend? The man was a *fool* and she was tempted to tell him so.

"No, thank you. I wouldn't *dream* of it. Anyway, your car is only meant for two."

He looked affronted. "I think you misunderstood. I could drive you home and then meet the others at the restaurant. It's no great distance and I'd probably be back before the food arrived."

Somehow that seemed even worse! As if he couldn't wait to dispose of the miserable killjoy who threatened to spoil his lovely evening. She noticed he had not been one of the ones who had tried to persuade her to stay. When she recovered the power of speech, she again made it absolutely clear that his offer was unnecessary and unacceptable.

As she sat alone in the back of her taxi, homeward-bound at last, she marveled over Nicholas's motives and this insulting display of insensitivity to both herself and Antoinette. It was so completely out of character with everything she knew of him that she could make no sense of it at all.

Her anger with him soon evaporated however as she ran through the scene again in her mind. When she had refused to join them everyone had made a fuss, tried to persuade her against her wishes, or annoyed her by offering to sacrifice their own plans. Only Nicholas had unobtrusively accepted her wishes and tried to help her achieve them. His offer, she realized in the end, was a simple act of kindness. And as for him being with another woman, what else could she expect? She was mature enough to accept that a man like Nicholas had never been and never would be short of girlfriends. He wasn't to know that she would be at the wine bar.

At least that ordeal is over, she told herself. He could parade as many beautiful blondes as he liked in front of her now and it could never hurt as much again.

Giles's 'few days' stretched to two weeks and Julie's examination loomed ever closer. It had become the focal point of her existence, hovering like a thunderstorm on the horizon. She studied and fretted and several times a week sought consolation in tending her parents' grave. On each visit she added topsoil, but by the following visit the earth looked the same, arid and thin and lifeless. She realized it would offer no nourishment to any kind of plant, not even a weed.

"I'm like Robert the Bruce's spider," she muttered one day, raking through the dry, undernourished earth with her fingers. "Each visit I have to start all over again. What am I doing wrong?"

She realized with sudden clarity that the footsteps of which she had been vaguely aware on the gravel path behind her had halted and that she was not alone. Warily, she turned to see Nicholas kneeling beside her, his face so close that, without losing her balance she might have been able to reach across and kiss him—had she been foolish enough to attempt it. Oh, but the temptation to do so was very nearly overwhelming and she found it difficult to breathe normally.

"It's the shade from this plane tree," he explained, rubbing the soil through his fingers. "There's no moisture here."

She gazed at his beautiful hands, his long, sensuous fingers and fought an overwhelming urge to seize them in hers and hold them to her cheek and lips, to nibble and kiss each finger one by one...feel them touching her, caressing her, just as they used to. His beautiful gardening hands, if only that was all they had been. If only it had been so simple. She tried to cure herself by imagining them doing intimate things to Antoinette's body. The punishing thought almost brought tears to her eyes.

"What can I *do?*" Her voice shook with emotion, her eyes still on his hands, mesmerized by them. "I wanted to plant some flowers."

"You'll need a lot more of this," he replied, patting the dry topsoil. "And plenty of water. Do you water it each time you add more soil?"

She shook her head slowly. "I didn't realize I needed to," she confessed. "I've never been any good with gardening." Or anything else, for that matter, she thought.

He smiled. Not the cool, polite smile she had grown to know recently but the old one. Or very nearly. "I'll get some water now."

She watched him walk to the nearby faucet and fill two plastic containers with water. His kindness brought an aching lump to her throat. She suddenly thought of Liz and wondered whether his kindness might be directed at Liz. After all, the grave belonged to Liz's parents too and she knew Liz had begun to feel guilty for not having tended to it in the past. Maybe she had asked Nicholas to take a look at it? Perhaps he was merely living up to his Good Samaritan reputation and had set himself a weekly quota of good deeds? Or perhaps he simply enjoyed performing acts of kindness? When he wasn't being unspeakably cruel, that was. *Is he doing this to hurt me? Killing me with kindness, maybe?* Who said that anyway? Shakespeare, probably—he seemed to have said everything else. Does he even care? The questions made her feel wretched.

"What should I plant?" she asked as he carefully distributed the water evenly over the rectangle of earth.

"What do you think they would like?"

She turned towards the headstone, gazing at the inscription for inspiration. She was beginning to find this whole game too painful.

"Oh Nicholas, I don't even know what flowers they cared for. I know so little about them." Her eyes began to mist with emotion and he helped her to her feet. "Mrs Bottomley says we'll have flowers all year round in our garden. I just wanted them to have the same."

"Then I'll pick something out for you and send one of the boys up with more topsoil."

He was still holding onto her arm and she looked at him, almost despairingly.

"Why are you always so kind?" she demanded, fighting back the tears. "Why do you *do* it?"

Their eyes met for an instant but he was guarded, his mask of indifference firmly back in place. He shrugged and looked off into the distance as they began to walk back to the cemetery gate along one of the narrow gravel paths between the rows of graves, many of which were adorned with huge flowers in their many autumnal shades of rust and yellow.

"It's nothing," he replied dismissively and they walked the rest of the way in silence, leaving Julie wrestling with her emotions. She wanted to shout, 'But it *is*! It *is*! How can I *bear* your kindness when I know you have such a *low* opinion of me?'

On the way he enquired about her headache of the other night and she took the opportunity to apologize for her churlishness and thank him for the offer of the lift home. She wanted to make him realize that she understood his motive and regretted having been so ungrateful. He looked surprised and threw her a sideways, quizzical look as if not sure whether to believe she really meant what she said.

He really hates me, she thought. He didn't trust anything she said. And why should he, given her history? At the cars they stopped again and Julie pulled out her keys from the pocket of her jacket. She threw a weak smile in the direction of the sleek blue car.

"So you extended your kindness to your Japanese friend, I see. Don't you miss your Ferrari, though? I thought red suited you so well."

He looked at her curiously. "You said you thought it was unimaginative," he corrected her. "And I believe once you called the color common."

Caught in another lie, but she could not resist muttering, "Only because of Annabel Campbell-Turner."

"Who?"

Julie smiled faintly. *Right answer.* "Never mind. How does Antoinette like the new color?" she asked boldly.

He shrugged his shoulders. "I haven't asked her." He watched her as she turned to unlock her car door. "So how is your...Welsh friend enjoying our little town?"

"Giles, you mean? Oh yes, I think he's enjoyed his time here. I haven't really asked him. I believe he's planning to leave tomorrow, actually."

"I expect you'll miss him?" His tone was neutral.

"Me? Oh I shouldn't think *I* will since I so seldom see him these days." Then a thought struck her, and a tiny flash of mischief prompted her on. "But I rather suspect *Liz* might, though." There, now! If Nicholas *is* interested in Elizabeth, he will have to play his cards very soon. "Well, goodbye, Nicholas, and thank you again, for everything. Oh, and, give my regards to your...to Antoinette."

CHAPTER TEN

A few evenings later, Julie found herself alone with Alex Saunders, awaiting Elizabeth's return from a meeting about the new clinic.

"Honestly," Julie remarked, "they ought to name it the Elizabeth Somerville Clinic for all the work Lizzie's put into the wretched thing."

He smiled benignly. "Yes, she's certainly keen. I really should have been there myself tonight, but I do find meetings like that a terrible bore."

"Oh? I hadn't realized you were involved with it."

"Well, yes, ever since it was decided to add an out-patient annex to it as a gesture to the hospital, to show that we're all working towards the same common good, so to speak. And speaking of out-patients, were you pleased with your friend's state of mind when he left?"

"Giles? Oh yes. He was very much improved. I must say though, I rather expected some sort of announcement before he left."

"Concerning Elizabeth?"

"Well yes. I expect I'm just too romantic, but I thought those two were becoming something of an item."

He smiled genially, refusing to rise to the gossip challenge.

"And what about you, Julie? What plans have *you* made for the future?"

"Me?" she asked, surprised. "None, beyond this wretched exam."

"What about your career?"

Julie frowned. "I just want to get the exam out of the way, first."

"Some people think you're devoting too much attention to your studies and your parents' grave and too little to yourself."

"*Some people?* You mean Elizabeth does! Oh yes! Liz *would* think that about the grave, though I'm surprised she said that about the studying. I would have thought in her book, there's no such thing as too much. If I fail the exam, she'll say I didn't study enough. I can't win. Is that why you're here—to assess my emotional stability, now that you've finished with Giles? Am I to be your next project?"

"As you know, I'm here to see Elizabeth."

Julie jumped to her feet and paced the room angrily. "I'm growing tired of Liz's unceasing concern about my future. I wish she'd stick to her wretched clinic and let me work things out by myself and in my own way."

"That's usually the best way," he conceded with a smile. "But you've undergone a lot of emotional turmoil this year and you strike me as being a very unhappy young woman. A very *stubborn*, unhappy young woman, if I may say so."

"If you had to live with Elizabeth, *you'd* be stubborn," she muttered gloomily. "I'm so tired of following in other people's footsteps. Of striving to achieve other people's ambitions for me."

"Then why don't you do what *you* want, for a change?"

Julie sank into a chair and stared into the fire moodily.

"Well?"

She sighed and thought, I tried that too and look what a mess I made of it. "I don't seem to be very good at making the right decisions. All my life people have made decisions for me and I've blindly followed their directions. When someone else has planned out your life from birth, you learn not to question it. You just go along with it."

"And if Elizabeth's *unceasing concern* vanished, what would you choose to do then?"

She stared at him blankly. "I don't know any more. I really don't know."

"Your husband had a forceful personality and influenced you a great deal, I think?"

"Yes, I suppose so. He was rather like my sister." And my father too, she thought.

"Yet when you removed yourself from his influence, the first person you sought was Elizabeth," he pointed out.

Julie stared at him. "*Removed myself from his influence*? You sound like something from a Victorian novel, doctor! Do you think it was unnatural to return to my childhood home, of which, by the way, I own half, or are you trying to suggest that I have a weak, dependent personality?" she taunted.

"I don't know how strong your personality really is," he answered gently. "But Giles once mentioned that you'd appealed to some previously unplumbed paternal instinct in Simon that he found irresistible, so I assumed he was rather dominant. Tell me, when you were a child, how did you view your future then?

"I don't know." Julie didn't want to pursue this line of thought. How dare Giles discuss her and Simon like that? But she didn't want to think about Simon or Giles just then.

She turned back towards the fire, watching the flames lick the old apple logs. Someone had cut them into neat blocks and stacked them in the woodshed. She could hardly believe it was any of Nicholas's doing. It seemed almost cannibalistic, in a way, to be burning logs from the old tree on the drawing room fire. Another cremation. But they burnt very well and what else was to be done with them? She was reminded of the old swing... *Make me ride higher, mummy, higher*. Were these crackling, scented logs the branch that once, long ago, supported and delighted her so much?

Eventually she applied herself to his question. "I suppose like most little girls, I wanted to be like my mother," she confessed quietly at last.

"And when you met your husband, did he take over the role of your father?" he probed softly, gently.

"Oh God!" she cried. "That wasn't just a chance comment Giles made. You've discussed me with him in intimate detail! How *could* you? Very well, let's admit it. That's what I wanted, wasn't it? Someone to look after me, just as father looked after mother."

"Someone who had the same high expectations of you as well?" he pointed out.

"Meaning I chose him to balance my weakness? Do you always try to make every relationship fit in with your complex Freudian theories of human nature? Or do you just think we're all hell-bent on self-destruction?"

"Why do you say that?" he asked leaning forward, eyes gleaming in the firelight.

Julie drew in a long, trembling breath before speaking again. "My father was a caring person. He loved my mother. I don't believe he had excessively high expectations of her."

"No," Alex agreed, with almost maddening calmness. "But he had of his daughters, hadn't he? Can you remember your father showing you affection?"

"I'm sure he did and I can certainly remember my mother showing me plenty," she retorted angrily.

"Why do you think that is Julie? I mean, you were seven years old when you lost your mother and, what...eighteen, nineteen when your father died?"

"How do you know so much?"

"Oh come, Julie, I've known your sister for several years. Do you think the relentless driving force behind her wouldn't intrigue anyone who cared about her? People interest me. I enjoy puzzling them out."

"It wasn't a negative thing. Lizzie had a very *good* relationship with father. She could do no wrong in his eyes."

"As perceived by *your* eyes, perhaps not," he pointed out mildly.

Julie fell into silent contemplation again. Now here was a truly novel thought! Had Elizabeth ever suffered from feelings of inadequacy, the way she, Julie, had? Was that why Liz had worked so relentlessly at her career at the cost of all else until it had become the only way of life for her and, in her eyes, for her younger sister? There was no doubt in her mind that this was what Alex Saunders was hinting at. And then there was the other startling thought. She had never considered before how very much like her father Simon was in his remote kindness and his stubborn expectations of her. Did that mean that by marrying Simon, after her father had died, she was trying to repeat the pattern of her childhood? Had she substituted Simon for her father in order to win his approval... which her father had denied her? Had she really such a weak and self-effacing personality? Giles had called her a coward and a hypocrite while Nicholas had thrown a whole catalogue of insults at her, and every one of them true.

"Are you suggesting that I have some sort of...need...to punish myself? She was almost fearful of hearing his answer.

Alex had removed a pen from his pocket and what looked like a used envelope on which he appeared to have been doodling during Julie's self-absorption. He clicked the pen once or twice thoughtfully.

"Would you say that you have made a habit of putting yourself in..." Here he paused to search for the best word. *"Demanding* situations recently?"

Julie released a faintly hysterical giggle. "No wonder the surgeons call you trick cyclists. You never give answers, just ask more questions, taking people for a detour all around the houses!" They exchanged wry smiles. "I suppose I *may* have been looking for a father figure when I married Simon," she conceded slowly. "But I never thought for a moment that I was *willfully* punishing myself in choosing someone who had impossible expectations of me. And I know Simon didn't think that either. He was very kind. He was the best friend I had."

"If he was, then he should certainly not have married you," Alex said with a brutal honesty that took her by surprise.

"That's a horrible thing to say! It's so insulting!"

"I'm sorry. I don't want to insult you or him. I just want to help you see things more clearly."

"Oh, you've done that all right!" she said without humor. "You've made me feel completely worthless. Got any beds on your psychiatric ward, or shall I just nip upstairs and slash my wrists now?"

"Julie, you're far from worthless, but you're not very honest with yourself..."

"I do wish you wouldn't keep trying to spare my feelings!" she interrupted with a sardonic expression on her face.

"But as for punishing yourself, isn't that what all this studying is?"

"Tell that to the Royal College of Physicians! They set the standards. How else do you suggest I succeed in hospital medicine without the exam?"

"But you've told three people I know personally, and who, I should add, have all expressed their concern about you, that you want out of hospital practice and yet you are punishing yourself with this study regime without giving any thought about what purpose it will serve you. You've shut yourself away in more ways than one and the only pleasure you seem to allow yourself is tending your parents' grave. Don't *you* think your friends are justified in their concern?"

Julie jumped to her feet in agitation and paced the room for a moment. Alex Saunders was again prodding at her Achilles heel and it was beginning to feel very uncomfortable.

"I think that's enough psychobabble for one night, Dr Saunders. If you'll excuse me, I think I'd better go back to my books. I'm sure Elizabeth won't be much longer," she said, decisively.

"Very well, Julie. But if you can't accept yourself it seems reasonable not to expect others to do so, wouldn't you agree?"

Julie halted abruptly at the doorway and turned slowly.

"Three people?" she asked, glancing back at him. "You said *three* people had expressed concern?"

He gave a slight shrug, his face inscrutable in the dim glow of the fire. "I imagine *all* your friends are concerned."

She laughed hollowly.

"What friends? I'm surprised you've managed to find three!"

"Well, of course, I count your sister as your friend as she is extremely worried about you."

"Liz isn't my friend, she's my albatross," Julie muttered. "Who else? Three people I've told about wanting to give up medicine? There's Giles, of course and..." A long silence ensued but she stepped back into the room, coming up close to his chair and stood gazing down at him calmly. "Was it Liz who talked to you about the cemetery?"

He shook his head.

"So this little discussion wasn't instigated by Liz after all?"

"She was expecting me at the meeting. I thought I mentioned that. There are other people who are concerned about you, who feel you have erected barriers around yourself, made yourself unapproachable—which I found curious in the light of my own observations."

"How could you have 'observed' anything about me, when you were supposed to be watching Giles the whole time?" she demanded.

"Forgive me, it's a rather unsavory little habit of mine, like listening in to other people's conversations in restaurants. I'm a student of body language. I told you, people interest me."

Julie slowly returned to her chair, taking tiny steps to allow herself time to formulate her next question. "Did Nicholas actually consult you about me?" It was almost too painful to say his name out loud.

Alex smiled a broad and genuine smile of amusement. "Of course not. Psychiatrists do have friends you know. And friends chat about their concerns. With a little gentle prompting, sometimes."

"Is Nicholas really a friend of yours? How well do you know him?"

"Quite well actually. As a matter of fact I believe we share more than one mutual friend. But apart from all those tedious meetings we've had to attend about the clinic, we do occasionally manage to get together socially," he said with measured understatement. "He's an excellent chap, Nicholas. First rate. Knows his own mind in most respects, too. I'd say he very rarely makes mistakes, though he admitted to making quite a painful blunder recently."

Julie sat back in her seat, resting her cheek against the chair back, concentrating on her breathing to keep it regular and watching Alex silently, waiting for him to elaborate.

"And it seems that every move he's made to put things right has been rejected. Of course in this case, there were misunderstandings on both sides—some of which I was able to help with. Or at least, to give an opinion about."

"Based on your observations?"

"And on personal knowledge. For example, *I* knew that your friendship with Giles was purely platonic."

"Oh really?" Julie smiled in delight. "And you worked that out from our body language?"

"No. I asked Liz. And Giles. Asked him at our first meeting, actually. Having seen you and Nicholas together it was clear to me that if Giles was in love with you, then it was certainly unrequited." Alex took on a pensive expression for a moment. "Interesting word that, don't you think? No-one ever talks about love being requited, only of it being *un*requited. Unrequited love gives off the plainest body language in the world. It's when it is requited that the language sometimes gets complicated. And I'm not just talking body language. Harder to read with any certainty, I mean. By everyone concerned. Which in turn causes so many misunderstandings. But then if you find it so difficult to love yourself, it may be hard to show your love... or accept that someone really does love you."

After Elizabeth arrived, Julie escaped to her room to be alone with her thoughts. And what thoughts they were as they teamed through her brain like powerful floodwaters. *Accept that someone really does love you.* Surely he couldn't mean Nicholas? It was very clear indeed to her that Nicholas was no longer interested in her and had moved on with his life. Alex must just mean that Nicholas no longer bore her any ill will. That he didn't want to see her continuing to suffer and pine, now that he'd been able to move on with his life. That he wanted her to be able to do the same. She should have known Nicholas wasn't the sort of person to bear grudges.

*Every move he's made to put things right has been rejected...*how could that be? True he did come to London after her, but surely that was on Sonya's behalf? Hadn't Sonya said as much in her letter? Julie now wished she had not thrown the note away, so she could read it again and satisfy her mind. He was just being a good friend to Robert and Sonya—after all, he was their best man and it was his job to see that the wedding went smoothly.

Nicholas had told Alex he had made a 'painful blunder'—could that have been...? No! He must have meant in assuming that she and Giles had some sort of romantic attachment. That was not an unreasonable mistake, given Giles's familiarity with her. She shuddered slightly at the memory of Giles's seemingly affectionate—and completely unwanted—gestures. Could Nicholas have been...was it even remotely possible that Nicholas had been jealous of Giles? Happy thought...but impossible!

You've made yourself unapproachable. Have I, Julie wondered, is that how I appear to him? *Erected barriers?* Maybe she had—for self-preservation, of course, because the pain would be just too much to go through again. *No, I could never put myself in that situation again!*

So how was she to handle all this new found information? How could she let her hopes soar, as they were doing right now, if she was mistaken...if Alex was mistaken? She would rather die than have to endure so much pain again, if she was wrong. She could not, *would* not let her hopes run away with her. She *had* to control herself and put Alex's suggestions right out of her mind so that the next time she saw Nicholas she would be cool, calm and collected and in a better position to observe him objectively and save herself, and him, from unnecessary embarrassment. The one thing she must *not* do was to throw herself at Nicholas and face rejection a second time.

She sat for all of five minutes, firm in her new resolve, before jumping to her feet.

She showered quickly, repeating *cool, calm and collected* to herself in much the same way Dorothy in *The Wizard of Oz* repeated, 'There's no place like home'. She barely dried herself before dressing and leaving the house. Her drive to The Cedars didn't take long at that time of night. Nevertheless, by the time she arrived, it was too dark to see much of the grounds as she drove towards the house. She stopped the car before reaching the front of the building. She picked her way along the drive, where the hedgerows were lit with dim solar lights, nestling low to the ground and casting only faint illumination along the path. It was like walking through a fairy grotto.

At the door, she paused. One or two dangly-legged crane flies hovered hopefully around the light. *I can't do this! What if I'm making a terrible mistake?* Breathe deeply, she reminded herself. She rang the doorbell, nervously, unsure whether she would find him alone, or even at home. Visions of finding him in the arms of Antoinette or some Annabel or Livvie almost impelled her to run while she had the chance. Perhaps she should have called first? If only to give him to opportunity to make an excuse. *Cool, calm and collected.* She trembled in the fragrant night air as she waited feeling anything but cool or calm and certainly not at all collected.

He answered the door himself and uttered her name in surprise.

"You said I might contact you if I needed anything," she reminded him, not knowing from where she had found the strength to speak, when all she wanted to do was throw her arms around him and tell him over and over how much she loved him.

"Yes, of course. What is it?" He seemed, for once, uncertain how to respond, even glancing beyond her as if expecting to see some sort of physical danger looming up behind her in the twilight gloom.

"Two very small things," she replied, pulling her left hand out from behind her back and handing him a bottle of champagne. "I need you to accept this small token of thanks from me for your kindness, to drink a toast to your new house. May it be the happiest home you've ever had, and also give you the best garden in the world."

He said nothing, but nodded slightly and accepted the bottle she held out, the shadow of a smile beginning to play at the outer corners of his mouth.

He hadn't refused it, was that a good sign? She took another deep breath and managed to quell the tremor from her voice as she continued.

"And..." Removing her right hand, she held forth a branch.

"What's this?" he asked, his face a picture of bewilderment.

"Tut, tut, call yourself a gardener?" she chided. "It's an olive branch, of course."

He shook his head. "That's not olive."

"And whose fault it that? I blame the gardener for not knowing I would need an olive tree, and I intend to talk to him severely for being so remiss. So I had to find the next best thing —a metaphorical olive branch." She waved it in front of him. "It's a cutting from our old apple tree. It's a wonderful old tree—been through such a lot but still hanging in there. *So long lives this and this gives life to thee*," she quoted solemnly, hoping he would remember, but he still didn't speak, just looked from her to the twig. "You can do a lot worse than have an apple tree in your garden. In fact, the best garden in the world must always have an apple tree in it." She stopped because she had run out of breath.

There was still no response and she bit her lip as she waited a moment before half turning towards the door. Either Alex was wrong or she had offended Nicholas by referring to things lacking in his childhood. Either way, it was a silly gesture and she had once again made a fool of herself. She had said her piece and said it badly, as usual. She might have profited from spending a year or so rehearsing it, she thought.

He looked at the twig doubtfully. "There's a couple of old cedars out there which will probably get very jealous, but, what the hell. They'll survive a bit of sibling rivalry." He held out his hand.

"Oh, Nicholas! What I was trying to say was that even if you can't forgive me, even if you can't accept my apologies, at least accept my gratitude. At least let me say thank you to you for all you've done, so that I can perhaps feel a little less wretched and a little bit hopeful that one day you'll be able to stop hating me and perhaps think of me as a friend.

"It doesn't seem fair to me," she went on sadly, "that you seem to be everyone else's friend but mine." She wanted to say more, but her voice had become dangerously husky and she knew she couldn't trust it with any more declarations right now.

"Would you close the door behind you, please?" he said finally, looking around for somewhere to deposit the twig.

Julie felt as if a jagged bolt of electricity had ripped through her body. *Rejection*? *Is he telling me to leave?* Gasping in pain, she turned towards the door and was about to step through it when he caught her arm, preventing her exit.

"Julie..."

She blinked back a tear as she turned to face him again.

"Where do you think you're going?"

"Home, of course."

"But I thought you came to see the house? Now close that door before any more of those damned crane flies get in and come inside properly so I can give you a tour."

Relief washed over her and she smiled through misty eyes. "No need. I've seen it already."

"What?"

"In my imagination," she explained. "It's a beautiful house."

"Not really. It still needs some vital work."

She looked beyond him at the light glowing out from one of the rooms. She wondered if Antoinette was hiding in there.

THE APPLE TREE

"Is it something serious?"

"What Sonya would call 'soul repair'. Can't you sense how empty it feels inside? Or is that just me?" He took a step forward and caught her suddenly in his arms. Their lips found each other immediately and the kiss they shared, lingering and sweeter than any before, was everything she had yearned for through all her hurt and pain and grief. It was the best kind of therapy and she felt its warmth and healing powers flood through her body and begin to make her feel whole again. She experienced again the same total sense of belonging and rightness which being with Nicholas always seemed to create, as if all the events of her life were a pale and insignificant backdrop to this moment, this critical core of her existence.

When they finally, reluctantly, drew apart he led her into the house, through the hallway and into the spacious living room softly illuminated by floor lamps and wall lights. The tall windows had their filmy drapes tied back to reveal pools of silvery light twinkling all the way down the long lawns of the lovely garden from numerous small solar lights, which lent it a fairytale appearance.

"It's a beautiful room, Nicholas," she breathed in delight, looking around her, absorbing everything greedily with her eyes while her body still tingled from his touch. And not an Antoinette in sight! "The best! And the garden looks like wonderland—it's absolutely perfect!"

"Well yes, true—it's much better *now*, I must admit, but it still needs some work...just like you and me. But I'm pretty sure we'll get there this time." He had not let go of her hand and now he drew her gently towards him again.

She felt like she was being reeled in, pulled back together, to where she belonged and could become complete again. She was home at last. When his lips claimed hers, she returned his kiss hungrily, holding nothing back from him. She would not allow him to doubt the depth and sincerity of her feelings.

When he finally pulled away, he gazed into her eyes for a long moment before speaking. "I love you, Julie, though I know I should hate you for putting me through hell these past months." He was prevented from continuing by the kisses she rained on his face, but seemed not to mind the interruption. "Those things I said to you that night," he resumed, shaking his head regretfully. "They may have hurt you a little, but they can't possibly have made you suffer more than you made me by just leaving like that! I almost went out of my mind then. It never occurred to me that you'd do that," he shook his head ruefully. "For one thing, I must admit, I didn't think you had the strength."

"To run away?" she asked in surprise. "Oh Nicholas, believe me that takes no strength at all—perhaps that's why I'm so good at it! You're wrong to think I wasn't hurt by what you said, the truth usually is painful. I should know! I feel as if all my life I've had to hide something about myself from someone important because I feared their rejection or I was afraid of hurting them. And the fact of having been married seemed both desperately trivial and desperately important and I didn't know how to tell you. Especially in light of the Masserman Manifesto."

He smiled and led her over to a vast pearl-grey leather sofa, spilling over with plump cushions, in front of a crackling log fire. "Oh *that*! You'll be glad to know that went into the shredding machine the day you left. And I almost joined it!"

"What are you saying, Nicholas?"

"That it's an extremely efficient machine. Bring your books over tomorrow and I'll prove it."

She smiled uncertainly. "That's a tempting proposition, but I'm not sure about that yet. Let's put that discussion on hold for now."

"Whatever you say. But you'll never specialize in cardiology with my blessing."

She laughed. "Good! I've been toying with the idea of going into general practice. I might make quite a good GP if I'm allowed just to be myself."

"I wouldn't want you to be anyone else."

"Or there's always teaching."

"Those who can..."

"Exactly! I could teach biology. It would only take a year to re-train. So you see there are lots of things I *could* be."

"Yes, there are. You *could* be my wife."

"I could? Do you really think I might qualify?"

"And the mother of my children."

She could no longer speak, only look at him with troubled, shining eyes.

"I could help you draft out your application form if you like," he went on.

"Sounds like a wonderful position," she said at last, unable to keep the tremor from her voice. "Do you think I have any chance of making the short list?"

"You *are* the short list, Julie. I haven't stopped loving you for an instant from the first moment I saw you and being apart from you again is unthinkable now. Marry me, Julie. Immediately. As soon as we possibly can. That's the only position I can bear to discuss with you right now. We belong together. And I think you know that as well as I do."

"Of course I do! I tried to tell you that the night of Robert's party, remember? Oh but..." She looked into the fireplace where the flames licked and sputtered around the banked up logs. A tidal wave of conflicting emotions surged over her. "I'm not sure if I dare trust myself yet. I'm afraid of making another mistake and ruining your life. You're too good for me. Far too special...everyone keeps telling me..."

He suppressed her protestations with a kiss which lingered until her resolve to make him understand her weaknesses extinguished itself.

She watched him adoringly, her head resting on the soft, silk cushions as he unfastened the wire bonnet of the champagne bottle and popped the cork under the gentle persuasion of his thumb, exactly as it should be done. He poured out the champagne and handed her a glass. She took a tiny sip and sighed.

"I don't have your strength of character, Nicholas. I shall probably be uncontrollably jealous of the Antoinettes, the Livvies and the Annabels in your life. I have a weak and dependent personality—you ask Alex Saunders...oh, but then I forgot, you already did."

Nicholas had the grace to look slightly sheepish as he took a sip of his champagne before returning his glass to the table.

"I admit it. I was suspicious and jealous about Giles Fairchild and I had to find out what the real situation was. It was that remark of yours the other day, at the cemetery that gave me the first ray of hope in months. So I asked Alex and...you know the rest."

"I'm ashamed of you for thinking I could ever be interested in someone like Giles, after you," she rebuked.

"And I'm ashamed of you for thinking I could ever be interested in someone like that estate agent before *or* after you!" he retorted.

"I never really did," she confessed. "It was Liz I was *really* worried about!"

After they had recovered from their laughter, and kissed some more, he told her soberly how he had come after her on the night of the party and of his shock on hearing she had left for London. Eventually he had tracked Elizabeth down and she had given him the telephone number, which he had called only to hear Simon's voice on the answering machine and promptly rung off.

"He sounded so *proprietorial*. I just couldn't bring myself to leave a message, because that was to acknowledge him. I thought, she's got an entire history with this man that I know nothing about," he explained, with a slow shake of his head. "And that thought nearly drove me insane."

Following that he had called several times without any answer until Simon's mother had answered the telephone and told him Julie was with Simon. "Only she never mentioned anything about his illness. I suppose she must have assumed I knew. It was Elizabeth who told me how seriously ill he was. And happened to mention what a mistake your marriage had been from the outset."

"But no-one told me any of this. Oh Nicholas, if only I'd known!" She thought of all the pain that could have been avoided just by knowing he still cared about her and how much she in her turn could have reassured him. She shook her head sadly, then took his hand in hers and began to kiss his beautiful fingers one by one, as she had longed to do so many times.

"I went to London before Liz went abroad, but you weren't at the house and you ignored my messages—that's assuming you got them. Do you realize how much of this might have been avoided if you'd only carry a phone?" he went on, letting his fingertips dance gently and tantalizingly over her lips as he spoke. "I didn't know what to think. The best case scenario was that you were punishing me, the worst that you were back with your husband. It wasn't until Sonya told me at the wedding what had happened that I began to piece things together. I hardly dared hope to be right, but when she told me we'd chosen the same tables, and insisted it was a sign, I let myself start to hope again! But you seemed so altered and aloof, as if you couldn't stand to be near me. Then Giles Fairchild turned up with his "Jules" this and "Jules" that and that really sickened me."

"Wretched man! I'm so sorry," she soothed, nibbling gently at his fingertips.

"So you should be! I very nearly committed a serious crime. And every time we met, you seemed to go out of your way to cut me or snub me...that night in the wine bar...I decided you really must hate me."

"I just couldn't bear seeing you with Antoinette!"

After assuring her that Antoinette meant nothing, which was a slow and deeply passionate process, and receiving her assurances that she had been so miserable without him that whenever she did see him she was rendered speechless and clumsy, he said, "There's still one thing I need to know, before I can totally forgive you. Do you remember telling me you loved me?"

"How could I forget?"

"And do you still?"

She moaned. "Yes, oh yes, of *course* I do. How can you doubt it? I've loved you ever since you were a struggling gardener, putting in a bit of overtime on early-closing day. But..."

"Forget the 'but', I was only interested in the 'yes'. After what you've put me through, I think I can manage the rest myself."

"I don't understand what happened to all those principles?"

He started to kiss her neck, his lips working their way slowly, sensuously to her left ear and down along her throat.

"Sometimes principles have to be re-evaluated in the light of events, if you are to move with the times. Sometimes people underestimate the strength of their emotions. They simply make mistakes, I suppose," he teased.

"Not you. Never!" she said, returning his kisses.

"Why not? I'm not perfect."

"Oh yes, you are, Nicholas. Why else would I love you so much?" she said fervently. Then later, carefully, anxiously, she asked, "You realize that, it's still a bit early for marriage—after Simon's death, I mean?

"Is it?" He sounded wary again.

"I mean I'll have to wait...just a little bit longer, don't you agree?"

"No," he amended. "*We'll* have to wait...together. Very, very much together from now on."

She let her head fall back again into the cushions again in order to enjoy his lovely face and smile into his eyes.

"Then I think I can safely promise that I'll give the position my most serious consideration," she whispered in his ear.

"And I can safely promise you that I intend to make sure you do exactly that," he replied solemnly. "Now, as you've expressed such an interest in the position, I think we should adjourn to the master bedroom to start drafting out that application I mentioned."

ABOUT THE AUTHOR

A former English teacher and head of department in a busy London school, Lynette gave up teaching two years ago to focus on her writing. Starting out as a freelance writer and editor to support her creative writing endeavors, she wrote her first contemporary romance 'The Apple Tree' which was awarded first prize in Inspired Romance's romantic story writing competition in December 2011.

Her second contemporary romance 'Wishful Thinking', released in April 2012, became a No. 1 seller in the UK Amazon's Kindle lists Romance category within its first week. Her romantic suspense, 'In Loving Hate', is due for publication in October 2012.

You can find out more about Lynette on her blog: http://manicscribbler.blogspot.com or through Facebook (Facebook.com/LynSofras) or Twitter (Twitter.com/ManicScribbler).

Thank you for your purchase.

We hope you've enjoyed your read and invite you to visit us
online for more sweet and inspirational romance titles from
Inspired Romance Novels!

www.inspiredromancenovels.com

Made in the USA
Lexington, KY
06 July 2012